THE LONG WEEKEND

SAVITA KALHAN

THE LONG WEEKEND

ANDERSEN PRESS • LONDON

First published in 2008 by
ANDERSEN PRESS LIMITED,
20 Vauxhall Bridge Road, London SW1V 2SA

www.andersenpress.co.uk

Reprinted 2009

British Library Cataloguing in Publication Data available

ISBN 978 1 84270 846 0

Typeset by FiSH Books, Enfield, Middx
Printed and bound in Great Britain by CPI Bookmarque, Croydon, CR0 4TD

For Taghreed, without whom it would never have started.

And for Hish and Jad, without whom it would never have continued.

1

It's tough being the new kid, but when you're not the only one it's not so bad. The problem was Sam was always the new kid and always the only one. He'd moved schools four times and moved countries three times – and he was only eleven. That had to be a bit of a record. He should write to the *Guinness Book of World Records* and get them to enter it as a new category. He'd be famous. Not that he wanted to be famous, but it would have been a pretty cool thing to tell people.

Sam slumped into his chair, and unloaded his brand new school regulation rucksack. He wondered why they had to carry the great hulking thing when it only contained a couple of books and some worksheets at any one time. Still, at least it was Friday and he had the whole weekend in front of him, and better still, he was going over to Lloyd's. Yes, Sam had made a friend – Lloyd, who just happened to be the coolest kid in the class. He was into everything Sam was into – football, tennis, swimming, running. Oh, apart from rugby that is, which Sam couldn't get his head around, yet.

The morning passed in a blur, much like the rest of the week had, except that he'd only got lost once, which was a new personal best as he had been averaging five times –

ten if you counted afternoons too! Although the credit had to go to Lloyd, who had stuck around with him – and who had a much better sense of direction than he had!

He followed Lloyd into Mandela Hall and checked out the lunch menu. It was the usual stuff that every school Sam had ever been to served up on a Friday: fish in some shape or form (and this must have been a good school because the fish was battered fillets and not star shaped, or fish shaped, or finger shaped, or guess-the-shape!), and chips and beans, or the 'healthy option' of baked potato and salad. Sam guessed that maybe Jamie Oliver or some other trendy chef had been in and done his thing. Lloyd scoffed the lot without wasting any time and he was on to seconds before Sam had got through his first helping.

'Get a move on, Sam. We've got a game lined up,' Lloyd said through a mouthful of treacle pudding. 'If it tips it down, we'll get told to come in.'

Flecks of custard spattered the general area as he spoke, but the largest blob hit Sam's tie and dribbled down onto his shirt. Sam didn't really care, although he knew his mum might be a bit annoyed. Lloyd wasn't the neatest or tidiest person in the class, but he was his friend, and Sam liked him.

The first few days at school had been tough – especially the break times. Sam had kicked a stone around the playground, watching the other Year Sevens playing football and pretending he wasn't interested when really all he wanted was to be one of them. He hadn't managed to summon up the courage to ask if he could join in in case they'd said no. Then he'd got to know Lloyd and within the space of a day he was in the game. So the choice between football and sitting in the dining hall eating treacle pudding was a non-starter. He grabbed a muffin and a banana and stuffed them into his pocket for later.

'Ready?' Lloyd asked, wiping his mouth with his sleeve.

'Yeah, let's go and show 'em how it's done!' Sam replied with gusto.

Ten minutes into the game the ball went over the eight-foot-high school fence, and with the Deputy Head on playground duty no one was about to risk detention by scaling it. Then the rain came down and the kids scattered back to their classrooms.

'I'll let you have a go on my new Xbox when you come over to me next time,' Lloyd said on the way in. 'I've got tons of cool games for it too.'

'You've got the new Xbox! Wow!' Sam exclaimed. He'd already been told he'd never get one – not even a PlayStation, which *everyone* had by the time they were in Year One! 'Waste of time and good money,' his dad had said grumpily the last time Sam had asked – and every other time Sam had asked. He hadn't given up trying though. He'd probably ask his dad again at the weekend. There was still the outside chance the answer might be a yes.

Lloyd had everything; it didn't seem like it was a big deal in his house. He was getting a brand new top-of-the-range mobile phone for his next birthday – it was an iPod and mobile rolled into one. As soon as he got it he said Sam could have his iPod as he wouldn't need it any more. He'd already invited Sam to his birthday even though it wasn't until some time in February.

'Can't wait,' Sam gushed, and he really couldn't. 'But hang on a minute, I thought we were going to yours today.'

'I thought it was yours today.'

'So which one is it?'

'We'll find out when one or both sets of parents pick us up, won't we?' Lloyd laughed.

Nothing seemed to faze Lloyd. He took everything in his stride and he was good at everything. Not that Sam wasn't clever. His reports always said he was a bright kid, and he usually did pretty well in most subjects. But just not with the style and ease that Lloyd had.

Double Science, followed by PE, double English, and Reading took up the rest of the afternoon and when the bell blared at 3.55, waking him and the rest of the class up from their silent reading, or silent sleeping, as Sam called it, he threw his homework, his reading book and his pencil case into his rucksack and headed over to Lloyd's desk.

'Ready?' he asked him.

Lloyd looked up through his unruly mop of red hair. 'You bet! Let's get outta here.'

'Wish they'd hurry up. It's almost half past four,' Lloyd muttered. 'They're late and it won't be funny soon!'

'Yeah, it's freezing,' Sam added. He was shivering, but trying hard not to show it as Lloyd wasn't even wearing a coat – it was stuffed in his school bag as usual. Sam turned his collar up at the wind, and then gave it his back, but the wind cut through him anyway.

Lloyd had pulled his mobile phone out and was staring at it angrily. 'Useless piece of junk! Battery's always dead or dying! Where's your phone, Sam?'

That was the thing about mobile phones – they were useless if you didn't charge them up and it didn't matter if they were your basic model or the top of the range and able to perform every function you might possibly want and hundreds you definitely didn't need or even know were there. Lloyd probably only remembered to charge his phone when it was completely dead.

'Left it behind,' Sam said. He didn't feel like admitting that there was no way his dad was going to let him have one just yet. Sam had already been working on his mum though, and there was the slim possibility that he might get one in the summer.

The sky was overcast, with angry black clouds that seemed to be warning them that a drenching was not too far away. The school bus had gone, taking half the kids home, and the others had run for waiting cars, engines idling, as soon as they were let out. Others, who lived locally, had legged it as soon as the bell rang. No one wanted to be left hanging around outside an empty school on a Friday afternoon.

Soon, apart from Sam and Lloyd, there were only a few other kids waiting by the side of the road. One by one they were picked up until only Sam and Lloyd and one other kid were left. The clouds decided at that moment to open up and add to the boys' already dampened spirits by drenching them as they ran for cover under a tree.

Just then a car slowed down next to them and the back passenger door flew open.

'Get in quick!' the driver called out.

Sam was impressed. The car was huge, like one of those big flash Mercs you see ferrying celebrities and rock stars around. Sam knew Lloyd was pretty wealthy, but he hadn't realised his family was *that* rich. He knew Lloyd's dad was big in music, but he wasn't sure exactly what he did. Maybe he was a famous singer, or a producer, like Simon Cowell, or someone like that. There was a lot he didn't know about Lloyd, but that was okay as he was going to be in this school for a very long time. His parents had promised him and Tab – that was his older sister – that they had settled and wouldn't be moving for at least a few years. Sam believed them because they had never actually said that before, and because his mum had finally planted asparagus in the garden. Sam had looked it up in the *Grow Your Own Vegetables* book that was always sitting on the kitchen table. Asparagus takes a few years to grow, so that meant they would have to stay there for at least three years.

The car gleamed brilliant white against the darkening sky like a beacon calling 'come inside where it's warm and dry' – and that's what Sam did. He followed Lloyd in and slammed the door shut quickly to keep the rain out.

He sank back into the shiny, dark leather upholstery, and the car moved off with a soft purr and the barely audible click of the central locking. The rain rattled on the roof, but Sam didn't notice it – the inside of the car took all his attention. It was like being in some kind of spaceship – everything was sleek and expensive looking, even the door handles had a polished wood trim around them which matched the trim around the seats, and the CD player, and the DVD player. There were hundreds of other buttons, too, and Sam found it hard to resist pressing them all.

'You'll warm up soon,' Lloyd's dad said. 'Had a good day, boys?'

'Yes, sir,' Lloyd replied, buckling his seat belt.

Sam couldn't imagine calling his dad anything other than Dad. Sir seemed so formal, but he followed Lloyd's lead and said, 'Yes, sir,' and added, 'Thank you. Sir.'

An elbow in his side made him look at Lloyd, who was laughing silently at him. 'What?' he whispered with palms upraised, but he'd gone red with embarrassment, which made Lloyd double up with a fit of giggling.

'What's so funny? Do you want to share the joke?' Lloyd's dad asked.

Lloyd straightened up in his seat and pulled a poker face. 'Oh, it's nothing, sir. Boring for grown-ups. Kids' stuff, you know.'

'Well, here's something to keep you going. Help yourselves,' he said, tossing a bag into the back seat, 'and I'll put the window up, so you don't have to whisper all that 'kid stuff'. There's CDs and DVDs back there if you get bored.'

The window that divided the back section of the car from the front whooshed up, enclosing them in their own private den. Sam wished his dad was like this, and had a car like this with a DVD player in the back and enough room to lie down. You could practically *live* in a car like this.

The contents of the bag were another surprise. It was full of crisps, chocolates, sweets, fizzy drinks, and tons of other bad stuff. But the boys were in heaven. They gaped at each other, boggle-eyed in amazement, before diving into the junk food paradise.

Twenty minutes later, they'd eaten as much as they could manage without throwing up, which was a fair amount, and there was still enough stuff left in there for their whole class. Lloyd pressed play on the CD player and Busted blared out. Busted had busted up, but Sam still liked them anyway. For some reason he still knew all the lyrics, which was probably a bit sad, but he never admitted to it to anyone. It wouldn't have been cool.

Sam thought it might be okay to press some of those hundreds of buttons that he'd been resisting. He didn't think Lloyd's dad would mind. There was a whole panel that controlled the DVD and CD player, one that adjusted each of the seats individually, temperature controls for each section of the back, seat warmers, Sat Nav system, the list was endless. It was a state-of-the-art car and Sam was sure there wasn't another one like it in the whole world. He shook his head in awe.

'Totally wicked!' he shouted, above the blaring music.

'Yeah,' Lloyd yelled back between singing, or rather shouting, the lyrics of *In the Year 3000*.

Sam smiled: someone else, someone much cooler than him, knew all the lyrics too. He pulled open the drawer beneath the DVD player and discovered a whole collection of films, some he'd seen, and some that he'd wanted to see forever but that his parents had said he was too young for.

'Do you want to watch one of these?' he yelled to Lloyd.

Lloyd turned the music off and checked out the titles. He ignored all the animated stuff and went straight for anything that had a rating of eighteen. He selected one and said, 'What do you think? It's supposed to be a bit scary. Can you handle that?'

''Course I can!' Sam said indignantly.

Sam wasn't about to admit that he scared easily. When his parents went out and left him at home with Tab, she *always* found the scariest thing to watch on TV, and he always had to hide behind the sofa. Tab didn't find anything scary and Sam wished he'd inherited that gene instead of the blonde hair one, which he knew Tab would have died for.

Lloyd took the DVD out of its case and slid it into the player. He pressed play and slumped back with a bag of crisps in one hand and a Coke in the other. Sam followed his lead. If there was a really bad bit in the film at least he could pretend he was taking a long sip of Coke and that way he wouldn't have to see the screen, although he'd probably still hear the screams.

The film started with a phone ringing and a babysitter answering it, and Sam's heart sank. He'd seen clips of this film and knew he was going to hate every minute of it. He sneaked a glance at Lloyd, who was totally engrossed in it. Within ten minutes, the babysitter had been killed in the most gruesome way – and Lloyd had spilt half his Coke down his shirt. Sam had only narrowly managed to avoid the same fate by clamping the can to his mouth just before the killer jumped out of the shadows.

'Crap!' Lloyd muttered, rubbing at the brown stain with a soggy tissue.

Outside it was gloomy and the rain drummed steadily on the roof of the car. Sam wondered how far away from school Lloyd lived, and how much more of this film he could take. Not much, he decided.

'Wannna go back to playing music?' he asked.

'Yeah, all right. I've seen this film a thousand times anyway. They all die in the end!' he said, laughing.

Sam wasn't sure Lloyd had ever really seen the film, but he wasn't going to say anything, and Lloyd was probably right about the ending. Although Tab always said there was usually one survivor and that the killer never really got caught, or killed at the end, because then the director could make another film without having to find a new idea.

They put on Usher's new album, and messed around with the Sat Nav system, typing in all the addresses they knew, and several they made up, and getting the system to come up with a route.

'Do you live quite far?' Sam asked.

'Not really. Usually home in half an hour,' Lloyd said. 'I'll put my address in and the school's, and then you can see.'

Lloyd typed in his home address and the name of the road their school was on. 'See?'

'But that's nowhere near any countryside,' Sam said, glancing out of the window at the empty fields and woods beyond.

'I know that, goofball. Your turn.'

Sam typed in his address and waited for the screen to come up with a route. It usually took about twenty minutes for him to get home from school, and more like half an hour to get to school in the mornings. His house was on the edge of a little town just outside London. 'Best of both worlds,' his dad had said. 'We get a bit of fresh air, but the big smoke's not too far.' His dad was a senior partner in a very big international property development company and the head office was in central London, so he had to get the train every day, and he complained about it every day, too.

'So where are we?' Lloyd said, peering at the map.

'What?' Sam asked, baffled by the question.

'Where are we on the map? Don't worry if you can't find it,' Lloyd said. 'Keep forgetting you're new to the area. I'll show you some brilliant cycle runs. I go out with my dad on Sunday afternoons and we could arrange it so you can come with us. If you want to.'

'That'd be great,' Sam said. He looked out of the window at the countryside rushing past. His watch said half past five, which didn't sound right. He couldn't remember what time they were picked up, but it had been late. Very late. It was definitely way after half past four, but Sam couldn't remember exactly what time it was, or why that was important now.

'We go camping,' he said. 'We're going for the weekend during half-term. Do you think you'd be allowed to go?'

'Might be. I'll have to ask Mum and Dad,' Lloyd replied. He leaned forwards and pressed eject on the CD player. 'Bored of this album. What do you want next?'

'Ask him now,' Sam said.

'Um, never heard of that one,' Lloyd said, flicking through the pages of the compact disc holder. 'Who's it by?'

'No, I mean, ask your dad now,' Sam said. Maybe he'd spoken too quietly because Lloyd wasn't listening to a word. His head was still buried in the CD holder and he was singing song titles as he flipped through them.

'Right, this one's good.' He put the new CD in and pressed play, his head bobbing from side to side in time with the music.

'Ask him now.'

There was an edge to Sam's voice, a slight tremor that made Lloyd stop and look at him. 'My phone's dead, stupid. Remember? Anyway, what's up with you?'

Sam swallowed hard. His mouth had gone dry. He reached for his Coke and realised that his hands were shaking too much to pick the can up.

Outside it was practically dark. The rain beat down incessantly, but Sam's heart was beating faster, and louder.

'Sam?'

2

It was a decision made without thinking, Sam thought later. Much later. Sometimes those big moments creep up on you without you even knowing it, or recognising it. You just act. Or follow. You don't stop and think: Should I be doing this? Is this the right thing to do? Is this something I should think about?

'Sam?'

Lloyd's voice sounded incredibly muffled. He could barely hear him. Sam looked at him. He could see Lloyd's lips moving, but couldn't work out what he was saying. Maybe he'd caught an ear infection, or something, from being out in the wind and the rain, and that's why he couldn't hear.

Sam turned away from Lloyd and glanced out of the window. Well, at least the rain had stopped, and the sky was a bit brighter, or rather not quite as dark. It was strange how one minute it was summer and the days were long and endless and warm. You were allowed to play in the garden for hours and stay up really late, and parents didn't mind too much. Then suddenly it was autumn and within a week it was colder and darker, and if you didn't go to bed on time you'd get an earful. Sam used to quite like autumn, but he couldn't work out why now.

Hands grabbed him by the shoulders and wrenched him away from the window.

'Listen!' Lloyd shouted into his face.

Sam did try to listen, but it wasn't his fault his ears weren't working properly. He put a finger in each ear and rubbed vigorously. Had that helped? He tried listening again. Mm, not much. What was Lloyd saying? He knew it must be important, because his friend kept saying it over and over again. The music was still blaring out from the CD player, but Sam couldn't make out who was singing. He recognised the tune, though, and that meant his ears must be working a bit. He had to listen to Lloyd carefully. Focus, Sam, he told himself. And that reminded him of his dad. His dad always said that when they were out playing cricket. 'Come on now, Sam, focus. Focus on the ball. Don't take your eyes off it. Keep your position. Bat at the ready,' he would say, and then, 'Excellent hit!' whether it was or wasn't.

Sam focussed.

Gradually, he made out the words. Words he didn't particularly want to hear. Maybe that's why his ears weren't working properly. They knew he didn't want to hear what Lloyd was saying. But he heard the words, and once he'd heard them he couldn't get them out of his head.

'Isn't this your car we're riding in?'

It could have been the chorus to a good song. Sam

sang it over and over to himself. *Isn't this your car we're riding in? Isn't this your car we're riding in? Isn't this your car we're riding in?*

Shut up! He screamed inside his head. Shut up! Shut up! Shut up!

'No,' he answered. His voice was small and quiet, like the whisper of a mouse.

Lloyd's mouth fell open. Their eyes turned simultaneously towards the driver. The dividing window was still up between the front and the back of the car. All they could see was the back of his head. Slightly balding, dark hair, blue shirt collar, and maybe shiny leather jacket shoulders. That's all they could see.

Sam pressed the button that opened his window. It didn't work. Maybe it was stuck. He pressed it harder. It still didn't work. He jabbed it several times. Then he punched it with his fist. Nothing happened. He reached across Lloyd and pressed all the buttons on his side. None of them worked. He pushed at the knob that unlocked his door. It didn't work. He reached across Lloyd and tried to unlock his door, but it didn't budge either. He yanked at the door handle so hard it should have come off in his hand, but the door remained shut and the handle remained firmly attached to it.

He sat back in his seat. 'Child locks are on, I guess,' he said, breathing heavily from the exertion.

Lloyd didn't reply. Sam guessed Lloyd's ears were going through a non-hearing stage like his had. Except Lloyd's eyes were watering as well. He didn't want to look at Lloyd in case he caught the eye-watering infection off him.

He didn't want to cry. He just wanted to get out of the space capsule. He wanted to be in his mum's little run-around, which still had the wind-up windows and was covered in crumbs; or in his dad's brand-new Jag, which did have electric windows, but which you played with at your peril. (He had tried it once and after his dad had almost had a heart attack over it, Sam had thought that it was probably not a good idea to do it again).

Lloyd was taller than Sam, and tougher. Once he got over the not-being-able-to-hear-or-think-straight thing, he'd come up with a plan. Lloyd always had a plan, an idea, a game. That first week at school had been one of the best first weeks at a new school Sam had ever had, and it had all been down to Lloyd.

Sam glanced at his friend. He was taking a long time to get over it. He had taken refuge in the corner of the car, huddled deep into the back of the seat. And he seemed to have shrunk a bit, too. It looked as though it was going to take him a bit longer to get over it. Shock. That was the word. Or was it horror? Either or both would do.

Sam concentrated on looking out of the window. He was hoping to catch someone's attention, but there was no one around. A glimpse of a road name would have been good, too, as they could have tried to work out where they were. But there didn't seem to be any people, or houses or road names in the countryside. Just trees. And fields. And more trees and more fields.

All he needed was one person to be walking down the lane. That wasn't too much to ask for. One person, out walking their dog, to spot a kid calling for help from a big white shiny flash car. They'd call the police, there might be a chase as the driver might not stop, but in the end he'd be outmanoeuvred by the cops, and crash into a hedge where he'd hit his head on the steering wheel so hard that blood would pour from the gaping wound, but Sam and Lloyd would be fine as they had their seat belts on. The police would smash open the back of the car and take them home to their mums and dads. The End.

But there was no one out there. No blinking people, no blinking dogs that needed blinking walking. *Blinking* was his mum's word. She never used *bloody*, she always said *blinking*. Sam didn't know why that word had popped into his head, but it just had.

There was a signpost up ahead, and a fork in the road. Sam squinted and wondered where he'd put his glasses. He could just make out the words: Puddinsford to the right, Haresfield to the left. Which one would the driver take? And where on earth were Puddinsford and Haresfield, anyway? Maybe Lloyd would know.

Sam turned the music up a notch. He knew the driver couldn't hear them, but it seemed like the right thing to do.

'Have you heard of Puddinsford or Haresfield?' he whispered.

Lloyd looked at Sam blankly. Either he was still suffering from hearing loss, or he'd never heard of those places. The car had reached the fork and without any hesitation swung over to the right.

'Lloyd, think! Have you heard of them?' Sam hissed louder this time.

Lloyd shook his head. Not good, but at least his friend was getting his hearing back and that meant tough Lloyd would be back soon with a plan that would get them out of here. Or a really good explanation for the situation they were in.

'Looks like we're headed towards a place called Puddinsford,' Sam whispered.

And then he had an idea.

'Hey, Lloyd, maybe your dad arranged a special treat for us. You know, like you told me he does sometimes. Like tickets to a concert, and meeting a famous pop star, or jamming with a band. He knows lots of famous people, doesn't he? All of them would have a car like this for sure. Who wouldn't if they had buckets of dosh?'

Sam was immensely pleased with himself. There was nothing to worry about. In fact there was everything to be excited about. Lloyd's dad had obviously organised something because he knew Lloyd wanted to impress his new friend. That had to be it. He rattled on for a bit about who he thought they were going to meet before he noticed that his coat sleeve was being tugged insistently.

'Yeah?' he said, turning to face Lloyd.

Before Lloyd could say anything the dividing window whooshed down for the first time during the journey.

'Be there in a couple of minutes,' the driver called back. 'Hope you're both comfortable. VIP treatment all the way for you two! And wait till you see what's in store for you. Stuff of dreams!'

The driver didn't wait for a reply. The dividing window slid back up, leaving the boys listening to Christina Aguilera's new album. Lloyd was not at all embarrassed at admitting that he was madly in love with her. If Sam ever said anything like that, the whole class would have rolled around laughing at him. But not at Lloyd.

'See, I told you! Your dad's brilliant, Lloyd, he's sorted this all out for us,' Sam gushed. 'Anyway, what were you going to say?'

'I think I'm going to be sick.'

Now that Sam looked at him properly, he thought that Lloyd did actually look a bit green. He looked for something for Lloyd to use and spotted the sweet bag. He dumped its contents on the opposite seats and handed the empty bag to Lloyd – just in time as it happened. Sam turned away and tried not to retch as the pungent smell filled the back of the car. He wished he could open the windows and get some fresh air in. He knew he had to do something – holding his breath wasn't working and pretty soon he'd have to ask Lloyd for the bag back and add the contents of his stomach to it as well. He rummaged through the pile of sweets until he found some extra strong mints and popped one in his mouth. When Lloyd had finished, Sam passed him the packet, but Lloyd shook his head. He still looked green. His freckles were standing out on his pale skin so much that they looked like they were about to make a bid for freedom.

'Must be the excitement,' Sam said, grinning, 'or all those chocolates and sweets earlier! We should have stopped after the tenth one!' He laughed, but Lloyd still looked ill.

'Sam?' Lloyd said weakly. 'I-I hope you're right.'

'What do you mean? Of course I'm right. Once I had a whole Yorkie bar, a Mars bar, a packet of wine gums, and twenty cola bottles, and I had bellyache all night. I think I threw up, too.'

'Not about that, Sam.'

'What then?'

'You know.'

Maybe Sam did know what Lloyd was referring to, but he wasn't going to let himself think that way. He was really pleased with his quite brilliant explanation – and the driver had backed it up too. Hadn't he said 'VIP treatment' and 'Stuff of dreams'?

Yes, Sam had been a bit afraid before the driver spoke to them, just a bit, but not any more. Now it all made perfect sense.

Lloyd was just being a pain. He was just embarrassed because he'd chucked up in front of his friend. And he'd obviously had way too many surprises and special treats. Not that Sam hadn't had any. He usually got a special treat on or around his birthday – you couldn't consider it to be a surprise in any way, but it was still pretty good. Occasionally, out of the blue, his parents would surprise him with something, like the new bike when it hadn't even been his birthday.

The car pulled off the road and went bumpity bump down a narrow lane, which was little more than a track. Overgrown hedgerows on either side brushed up close against the car. Swish, swash, swish, swash – it was like being in the car wash with his dad, and just as claustrophobic. Most kids loved the car wash, but Sam was one of the few who hated it. He never admitted to it though, and so his dad always asked him if he wanted to go with him. Nowadays, homework usually provided the best reason for just not being able to go.

'Sorry, Dad, but I've got stacks of homework to get through,' he would say in a very convincingly resigned tone.

'Never mind, son. We'll go out and hit a few balls later when you're done,' his dad would reply, which suited Sam fine. Cricket versus car wash – no contest there.

Suddenly the car stopped. In front of them was a large wrought-iron gate. It swung open slowly, inviting them in.

3

What lay beyond the gates?

The excitement was almost too much to bear. Sam held his breath. It was almost completely dark outside now, and there were no lights up ahead. The driveway swung round in an arc for about half a mile, and then as they rounded a bend, they were almost upon it before they saw it. It was a huge, enormous house, well, more like a stately home or something. It could have housed hundreds of people, and probably did at one time. You must have had to be fabulously wealthy to own a great big heap like this, so it stood to reason that it had to be the home of someone very famous.

Sam looked askance at Lloyd, who just shrugged. He had no idea who lived here either.

The car sidled slowly towards the grand entrance where it came to a halt. Gleaming white pillars supported a portico with a row of cherubs sitting on top. The cherubs were dancing, all smiles and laughter, frozen in stone.

'Don't leave me on my own,' Lloyd said.

'What?' Sam said.

The driver had switched off the engine and was getting out of the car.

'Please, Sam, don't leave me on my own.' Lloyd's voice was barely more than a whisper. His face was in shadow, so Sam couldn't see his expression, but the whites of his eyes glowed iridescently, reflecting the porch light.

'I won't,' Sam promised his friend. 'We're going to have the best time ever, Lloyd. We're gonna have a blast!'

Sam's door opened and his heart beat just a little faster. His mouth had gone dry and he wished he had a long, tall glass of water. The excitement had got the better of him.

'Out you get then,' the driver instructed.

But Sam found that his legs had gone a bit jellylike, all wobbly and hard to control. Lloyd had infected him with his nerves. Get out of the car, you idiot, he cajoled himself. He couldn't see the driver's face as the man was standing back, holding the door open, but what caught his eye were the shiny, black, pointy boots that peeked out from beneath the black jeans the man was wearing. Strange things for a driver to be wearing, but, he supposed, if you had to drive around for pop stars all the time, you were bound to try to be a bit more trendy than regular people.

'Come on, I haven't got all day.' A note of irritation had crept into the man's voice, but when he continued all trace of it had gone. 'Got to get you two settled in and start the dinner before all the others get here.'

'All the others?' Sam said, finally regaining control over his legs and swinging them out of the car. It sounded like there was going to be a bit of a party.

Lloyd followed him out. He'd hidden the bag of sick in the car as Sam was getting out, just in case he got in trouble with the driver.

'I'll take you both straight to the room where you'll probably be spending most of your time – I know I'd be if I was a kid.' The man laughed, and didn't seem to notice that neither of the boys were laughing with him.

He slammed the car door shut and crunched across the gravel to the heavy wooden door. The boys swung their rucksacks over their backs and followed him.

'Nice car,' Lloyd said to the man, who was busy flicking through a key chain heavy with hundreds of keys.

Sam grinned at his friend happily. Lloyd had spoken, which meant that he must have been feeling a bit better. It had been getting a bit boring, but all that would change now that Lloyd had bucked up.

'Yeah, kids love it,' the man said distractedly. 'Ah, got it,' he said, and inserted a key into the lock, he turned it and then used the next key on the key chain to open another lock. 'Here we go,' the man said.

The door inched open with an aching groan and a dimly lit hall came slowly into view.

'After you, lads,' the man said.

Sam and Lloyd stepped inside together.

The hallway was an elaborate oak-panelled affair with hard wood flooring to match, a vaulted ceiling, and hundreds of portraits of white-haired old people who could have come straight off the walls of Hogwarts. The only relief came from the two very large mirrors on either side of them, but even those were enclosed within heavily gilded frames. The sharp smell of lemony furniture polish hung in the air, but it didn't mask the faint mustiness clinging to the walls.

The boys caught sight of themselves in the mirrors and their eyes met. They seemed to be saying something that their mouths couldn't. Behind them, the man dropped his bunch of keys and cursed. He fumbled around for the key fob and laboriously went through the whole process of finding the right key again so he could lock the front door. Lloyd stuck his tongue out at the mirror, like a kid half his age might do, but it made Sam grin nevertheless. Lloyd was back to himself.

They were led through the hall and up a flight of creaky old stairs to the first floor. Another long corridor faced them, lined with overstuffed bookcases and more ancient portraits, and then finally they reached another door. This time the man had the key ready and unlocked the door quickly.

'I should get you to close your eyes, but I think you'll be impressed enough. Besides, it's not like you're six year olds or anything.' He opened the door. 'Welcome to the

Pleasure Dome!' he said, beaming at them. 'Every kid's dream!'

Neither of the boys knew quite what to expect. In a house like this, they probably expected to see a musty old snooker room, or billiards room, which would have been fun for about five minutes as Sam and Lloyd weren't really into stuff like that.

They stepped cautiously into the room, and gasped. It was like nothing they had ever seen before – and definitely not in keeping with the rest of the house. Sam wondered whether Charlie had felt like this when he first entered Willy Wonka's Chocolate Factory. The room was practically the size of a football pitch and full of everything that any kid in his right mind would want for Christmas. The TV must have been the biggest one in England. It took up the whole of a very large wall. Sam turned his eyes away from it and let them feast on the rest of the room. Dotted around were things like a pinball machine, table football, a jukebox, a table-tennis table, and, unbelievably, a whole arcade of games, most of which Sam had never been allowed to play on because his parents disapproved of games arcades.

It was better than brilliant, and wicked, and cool and every other word that Sam knew, but Lloyd had taught him the new word for it, and this was one of those times when it was the perfect thing to say. 'Totally legend!' he breathed.

'With you there!' Lloyd exclaimed.

One of the other walls was lined with what looked like framed records, and pictures of famous bands and singers. Lloyd's dad *had* arranged it all for them – and this was just the beginning. It was all just as the man had said, 'stuff of dreams'.

'Make yourselves at home,' the man said. 'Play with anything you want, for as long as you want. I'll bring your dinner up in a bit.' He went out, leaving Sam and Lloyd alone in the room with every kid's dream.

'Dunno where to start,' Lloyd said, his eyes as big as footballs. He shook his head. 'Still can't believe Dad did all this, and he didn't let on about any of it!'

'Let's check out the games first,' Sam said. Not that he was anxious that it might all suddenly disappear and he'd never get to play on them.

'Okay. I know the good ones,' Lloyd said, leading the way.

An hour later, Sam's fingers were sore from pressing buttons like a maniac. It had taken him a while to get the hang of some of the games, but now he was a pro. Where was the nearest arcade to his house, he wondered? He didn't remember seeing any in his town. Maybe you could only find them at the seaside now. Lloyd would know. He would ask him when he finished this game. The only problem was that every time he set himself a goal, once he'd reached it, he'd set another one and so the game went on. He wasn't addicted to it or anything. He just found it hard to stop because it was way too much fun.

He did stop in the end, but that was because the man came back with a tray of food that smelled too good, and that made Sam and Lloyd realise that they were starving.

'Eat as much as you want. I'll be back in a bit,' he said, and left them to it.

Three different types of pizza, nuggets, sausages, chips, and a giant-size bottle of ketchup – kids' food. Junk food, his mum called it. She always made proper food with homemade sauces, and she loved to experiment. Some of the experiments had gone horribly wrong and even his mum had said 'yuck', but most of the time they were pretty good. Although, since Tab had become a vegetarian, they had all started eating less meat, and Sam struggled with that. When he was younger his dad had called him 'T-rex', or 'my little carnivore', and occasionally, very embarrassingly, he still did!

Sam speared his second sausage with his fork, dunked it liberally in his puddle of ketchup, and took a bite.

'Like a bit of sausage with your ketchup?' Lloyd said.

'I usually drink it out of the bottle,' Sam replied, going in for a second dunk, 'but it's not good manners to do that in public.'

'Hey, we forgot to ask the bloke when the others were arriving.'

'Oh yeah. We'll ask when he comes back for the tray.' Sam eyed the last sausage.

'Go on, you can have it,' Lloyd said. 'I can't stand them, and anyway, I'm full. Can't fit another thing in, and I'm desperate for the loo.'

'I need to go, too. Let's go and look for it. I'll eat this on the way.'

Lloyd led the way across the room, taking the longest route and weaving in and out of all the tables.

'Catch me if you can,' he called out before legging it, which turned it into a race with Lloyd getting there a split second before Sam.

'Beat you,' he chimed.

'Only because I was still eating!' Sam objected.

Lloyd turned the handle and pulled, but the door didn't open.

'Let me try,' Sam said, sticking the rest of the sausage in his mouth. 'It's really stuck!' Sam said, heaving as hard as he could. He stopped and looked at Lloyd. 'Or – or maybe it's locked, or something.'

'Why would he lock us in?'

'I dunno. Maybe there's another surprise and it would be ruined if we saw it.' As soon as Sam had said them, he knew how stupid his words sounded. They probably would have been okay if he was six, but he wasn't six, he was a very grown-up eleven. Even Lloyd was looking at him sceptically. 'Well, you think of a reason,' he said irritably.

Lloyd shrugged. 'Can't think of one. Unless he thinks we'll go snooping around and trash the house.'

'Or go exploring and get lost.'

'Or steal the family jewels,' Lloyd suggested.

'Or . . .' but Sam had run out of reasons.

'Or?' said Lloyd.

Neither of them said it, but they both thought it at exactly the same moment.

To keep us prisoner.

4

No, it couldn't be that. Not that, Sam reasoned. 'It's got to be something to do with the surprise ... Hasn't it?'

'Yeah, must be,' Lloyd agreed readily. 'Problem is, well, I'm really desperate!'

'How do we call him?' Sam wondered aloud.

'Beats me.'

They looked around the room again. It was chock-a-block with stuff, but neither of them had seen a phone or an intercom system when they had been exploring. They knew there had to be a way of getting in touch with the man for emergencies and stuff – like now. There were several windows running down the outside wall of the room, but they were too high up to look out of. Sam would have to climb onto Lloyd's shoulders to see out. All the other walls were covered in framed records and pictures, apart from one which the TV took up entirely.

'Look,' Sam said, pointing towards it.

'What?' Lloyd said, hopping from one foot to the other. 'I really need to go, Sam!'

'There's a door there, isn't there?'

'Oh yeah, looks like it. It'd better be a loo!' Lloyd said, zigzagging past the pinball machine and the table-tennis table. He turned the knob and the door opened. 'Kerching!' he exclaimed in relief. 'Me first!'

Sam leaned against the wall, waiting his turn. He was used to waiting. At home, he shared a bathroom with Tab and that meant a lot of waiting around on the landing, unless he timed it right – and either he rarely ever did or Tab spent all her time in the bathroom. His mum, in her wisdom, had put a bookcase right next to the bathroom door in a sneaky effort to get him to read more. Sam smiled to himself, because her plan had actually worked. He caught a movement out of the corner of his eye and glanced round. There was no one there. They must have knocked against the pool table on their way past and nudged the balls. The balls were still now.

'Hurry up!' he yelled at Lloyd.

'I'm trying,' Lloyd answered. His voice sounded muffled through the door.

There it was again. Something had moved. Sam let his eyes wander round the room, and then he looked up. He saw it, but didn't look at it for long. He pushed off from the wall and inspected the large collection of DVDs and videos on the shelves next to the TV. On the lower shelves were all the kiddies stuff like *Jungle Book*, *Bambi* and *Barney*, and some *Tweenies*. The middle shelves had stuff like *Toy Story*, and *The Incredibles*, and all the Harry Potters and even *A Series of Unfortunate Events*, which was one of Sam's favourite films. There were even some films there which Sam didn't think were out on DVD yet. The shelves above were full of 15s and 18s, and Sam hardly recognised any of them. There was a whole collection of videos with nothing written on them. Sam was reaching up to them when Lloyd came out of the bathroom with a grin on his face.

'You've got to see it! Wish I had a bathroom like that.'

'That's what I've been waiting for. You were *ages*,' Sam grumbled, pushing past Lloyd.

'Okay, okay, not my fault. It takes as long as it does, doesn't it?'

'Whatever,' Sam muttered. As he closed the door he glanced up, and a little red dot next to the eye seemed to wink at him. He slammed the door shut and locked it quickly.

Lloyd was right about the bathroom. You had to see it to believe it. It was all hard, shiny, pink marble and gleaming chrome, with a sunken bath right slap bang in the middle, surrounded by a thick deep white carpet. There was a whole stack of fluffy towels and little soaps set neatly on shiny chrome and glass shelves, and a row of porcelain animals, which looked completely out of place.

Sam almost took his shoes off before going any further, but he didn't. He really needed the loo, and somehow the thought of taking his shoes off made him feel a bit funny.

Vulnerable, that was probably the word for it. He had overheard his mum explaining his sister's recent mood swings to his dad. She had said, 'Tabitha's feeling a little vulnerable at the moment, Derek,' and Sam had thought that it was quite an interesting word, but until now he hadn't really understood its meaning. He didn't much care for it any more and couldn't understand why he'd liked it in the first place. It was actually quite horrible. Poor Tab, he thought. Now he knew how she felt.

He didn't look up into the corners of the room because he really needed a wee and that would have stopped him from being able to go. He finished much faster than Lloyd had and went and washed his hands. Whoever owned the house must have had an army of cleaners, Sam decided. He had never seen such a clean bathroom before, not that his wasn't clean, it was; but this was a different sort of clean. It was the kind of clean that something can only be when it's brand new and never been used before. He padded through the deep carpet back to the door and unlocked it. Only then did he risk a quick look up. His shoulders tensed, but it was okay as there was nothing there.

He caught sight of his face in the mirror and didn't know who it was for a minute, which felt a bit weird. His eyes were like black hollows and his face looked longer, kind of thin and gaunt. He was a bit skinny, he supposed, which was why his mum practically force-fed him at every meal. Well, she wasn't quite *that* bad, but she did make him have seconds at home, and pudding when she'd had time to make it. If he hadn't stopped and looked in the stupid mirror, he wouldn't have noticed it. But he had. In the corner of the mirror, a little red dot was reflected back at Sam. He turned and fled, slamming the door behind him.

Lloyd was at the pool table, rolling the balls up and down and off the side cushions at great speed in some kind of demented game. He stopped when he saw Sam coming out of the bathroom. 'What's up with you? You look like you've seen a ghost or something.'

'Don't know,' Sam replied, shrugging. He dug his hands deep inside his pockets, and leaned back against the jukebox, his back to the far corner of the room.

'Wanna play something?' Lloyd asked.

'Nah, don't feel like it. Lloyd?'

'Yeah?'

'I – I think we're being watched,' Sam said, his voice so quiet that he wasn't sure whether he had actually said the words out loud or thought them.

'What?'

'I said, I think we're being watched.'

'What do you mean?'

'Don't look up, but there's a camera on in the far corner. I said don't look!' Sam hissed angrily as Lloyd looked around for the camera in such an obvious way that if anyone was watching they would have known exactly what Lloyd was doing.

'Okay, okay. Take it easy. So what if there's a camera? We've got them too. It's like an alarm system or something, Dad said. And you'd need it in a room like this. This stuff must be worth a fortune. You wouldn't want anyone to nick it.'

'That's true, but there's one in the—' he lowered his voice to barely a murmur, 'in the bathroom, too.'

Lloyd looked doubtful at first, and then annoyed, very annoyed. His eyebrows knitted together and bore a macabre resemblance to a deep gash across the length of his forehead. 'No, there isn't! You're just trying to creep me out. Just shut up, will you?'

Sam shook his head. He felt wretched. 'I'm not, Lloyd, and there is one. I saw it.'

All the balls had come to a stop on the pool table, so Lloyd sent them whizzing round again. His hair had fallen over his eyes and Sam couldn't see his expression, or what he was thinking. Or whether he was thinking the same thoughts as Sam and that was why he couldn't trust himself to look up.

'There's probably a good reason for that, isn't there?' Sam said. 'You know, for that camera to be there?'

Lloyd racked up the balls on the pool table for a break and picked up the pool cue.

'Something to do with the alarm system, or something ...' Sam's voice trailed off.

Lloyd had not replied, but Sam could see that his hand was shaking hard and he could barely hold the cue, never mind line it up for a shot.

'But lots of things haven't added up,' Sam continued in a measured tone. He was actually amazed at himself for keeping his cool. 'Next time he comes in, we'll have to ask a few questions.'

'Without letting on what we ... what we suspect,' Lloyd added, and he whacked the white ball hard. It bounced off the table and rolled away.

What they suspected still had no name. Because really, Sam thought, it was just too silly. So it couldn't be that, or anything like that. Could it? Ever since they had come back to live in England his mum had been warning him and Tab about things like that. She would read about it in all the papers – the *Local Fright* was the worst paper, because it's on your doorstep, she would say. Life abroad had been very different. Cocooned. Protected. Easy. Sam had tried to tell Lloyd about it, but he hadn't really understood.

'Yeah, that's it. We could ask him about who he works for, and about all the other people who are supposed to be coming. No, I know, we'll ask him about music, bands and singers and stuff, because you know all about that.'

'And I'll know if he's lying,' Lloyd said, setting the cue down.

'But what if he knows all the right answers?'

'Then everything's fine, duh-brain! Isn't it?'

Sam wasn't so sure. 'Suppose so. And what if he ...' Sam was reluctant to finish his sentence. He didn't want to get Lloyd all upset and angry again, but at the same time they had to talk about a back-up plan, or something. He'd been hoping Lloyd would come up with one, but that wasn't happening. 'What if he *is* lying?'

The boys turned towards the door at the unmistakable sound of a key being turned in the lock, and the question was left hanging in the air, begging for an answer.

5

'All right, lads?' the man said in a bright, cheery voice.

He was acting normal, Sam thought. Maybe everything was normal. Maybe it was just him who had the heebie-jeebies.

'Yeah,' both boys answered simultaneously.

'I see you demolished the food. Still hungry?' he asked solicitously, kindly.

The boys shook their heads.

'I've got ice cream. And chocolate sauce. And all sorts of sprinkles,' he said playfully. 'Sure you don't want some?'

'No thanks,' Sam said.

'We're full to bursting. Thanks,' Lloyd added.

'When are the others coming?' Sam asked bluntly, going straight to the point, which wasn't what they had planned, but he couldn't help himself. He had to know.

'Others?' the man repeated, looking slightly perplexed for a moment. 'Oh, them,' he said in complete understanding. 'There's been a small change in plan. They got held up at a gig. They'll be here tomorrow, though.'

'Um, who's them, anyway?' Lloyd ventured.

'Didn't I say? Well, in that case, I think I'll leave it as another surprise for tomorrow. I'll just say one thing – they're recording a new album,' the man said, teasingly.

'Hey, that's not fair,' Lloyd objected. 'You can't say that and not tell us!'

'Oh, yes, I can,' the man laughed. His pale blue eyes crinkled up and disappeared when he laughed.

He seemed really friendly. Nice. But was he a wolf in sheep's clothing, or just an old sheep trying his hardest to be cool and trendy? Sam shook his head at himself – he was a lost cause. He was still sitting on the sidelines, still in denial, and almost as bad as Lloyd, who was getting carried away with the guessing game the man had initiated. Sam knew he should take charge of the investigation and get to the bottom of it. Friend or foe? Angel or demon? Which one is it? Which one was *he*?

Which one are you? he asked the man. But he hadn't said it aloud, because no one looked at him. Lloyd was still going through the top 100 chart list, and the man was having enormous fun saying no, or maybe, in response.

'Okay, I give up. You're gonna have to tell us,' Lloyd said.

'Can't do that, it would ruin it for you.'

'Did my dad tell you not to tell us? Because if so there's no need to worry. We won't let on that you let it slip. Honestly, you won't get into trouble, or anything,' Lloyd persisted in a wheedling tone.

Lloyd was really enjoying himself, Sam thought. He was almost jumping up and down with the anticipated excitement of meeting whoever was supposed to be showing up the next morning. It was perfectly clear that he thought the man was a trendy old sheep. Maybe he had already sussed the bloke out and knew he was okay. Maybe he had asked all the catch-you-out-questions, and hadn't caught him out. The man did seem to know tons about music – but when Sam thought about it, he hadn't actually said that much. He'd laughed a lot. It was Lloyd who was doing all the talking. So how did Lloyd know he was okay?

He didn't. He'd been sidetracked, as Sam's mother would have put it. She was always saying that about Sam. Sam could hear her warm, patient voice now, 'Don't digress so much, darling, you lose track of the point.' Which was true, Sam supposed. Well, his mum would have been proud of him now. He hadn't lost track.

The problem was how to get Lloyd back on track. He'd lost the plot completely, but he didn't have a clue about it. Sam would have to say something that snapped him out of it. The only thing was that Sam wasn't sure how to do that without alerting the man to the fact that they thought he might be a bit suspicious.

And then he had a brainwave. 'So can we come back tomorrow and meet them?' he said.

'Too far,' the man said, breezily. 'You might as well stick around. There's plenty of room, and it's all sorted with your parents.'

'Cool,' Lloyd said. 'Can't wait 'til tomorrow.'

Sam wished Lloyd would shut up or wake up. But he wasn't doing either. Open your eyes, you idiot, he's trying to fool you. Why do you believe him? Why don't I?

Sam wished he could communicate telepathically – but if he could do that maybe the man could do it too, and that would be worse, wouldn't it? You'd end up with strangers inside your head all the time, and someone would have to manufacture a pop-up blocker that blocked everyone else's thoughts from popping up in your head. When Sam thought about it, maybe telepathy wasn't such a great idea. And maybe this was exactly what Sam's mum meant about him digressing and losing track of the point. Focus, Sam. The man was talking again.

'Well, they might show up later tonight. No telling with these young – people. Almost let the cat out of the bag then, didn't I?' The man cackled. 'Tell you what, as you're so keen on meeting them, I'll wake you up when they arrive. How's that?'

'Brilliant!' Lloyd exclaimed.

'But you don't even know who they are!' Sam snapped. He hadn't meant it to come out like that, but it was too late, the words were out. The man looked at him appraisingly, and then raised an eyebrow. Lloyd hadn't even noticed. Not Sam's tone, and not the way the man had looked at him.

'I think I've got an idea about that,' Lloyd said, grinning at the man as though they shared a private secret.

When had it all changed? Sam didn't know. But it had. Maybe that's why Lloyd made friends so easily, because he was so open and trusting by nature. Sam wasn't going to let it go now, though. He had to make Lloyd aware of what was going on before ... before it didn't matter any more. 'Who is it then?' he demanded.

'Not telling,' Lloyd sang. 'I'm not gonna spoil the surprise for you,' he said, colluding with the man.

'You know I don't go in for surprises, Lloyd. I hate them. I'd rather know. Please.'

'You big liar! You said you love surprises!'

Sam could have hit him. But he didn't. *Obtuse* and *naïve* were two pretty good words that Sam's sister would have used then. Tab often sounded like a walking dictionary, unless she had friends over and then she sounded completely different. Lloyd was being those words so incredibly that if there had been a role for a Mr. Gullible in *The Incredibles* and Lloyd had auditioned for it, he would have got it hands down. In fact, if they'd known about Lloyd, they would have written the part into the film just for him.

'It's okay. Don't tell me. I'm not feeling that great anyway,' Sam said. He turned to the man and concentrated on speaking in a light, bantering non-suspicious way, which was extremely hard when the blood was pounding in your head, and everything looked wonky and kept tilting from side to side, and someone had set your mouth in cement and it felt all dry and stiff, and all you really wanted to do was to scream and scream. 'If you can't take me home tonight, could you call me a taxi or something. My parents will pay for it.'

'Don't be stupid, Sam!' It was Lloyd. Good old stupid, stupid Lloyd, who had replied.

'I'm not,' Sam said. '*I'm* not stupid!'

'Yes, you are. You can't miss the best part of the surprise. Dad'll be really upset. Especially as he went to so much effort for us to have the best time ever. For god's sake, Sam, get a grip, will you?'

The man remained silent, regarding Sam through his hooded eyes. A small smile played around his lips. He didn't have to say anything.

'But I just don't feel that great. I want to go home,' Sam said, forcing the words out with great difficulty. Someone had a hand inside his chest and was squeezing the air out of his lungs.

'Well, you can't,' Lloyd said, pouting. 'You're not gonna ruin this.'

'Now, now, boys. No need to come to blows over this. Listen, it's been a long night with too much excitement and you're both tired. Let me show you your rooms and you can have a sleep. Come on.'

Sam couldn't move. The cement must have dripped down his face and stuck his feet to the ground. Lloyd glared at him and yanked his arm hard. Sam didn't feel it.

He allowed himself to be dragged out of the bright room and into the dim corridor. All the way down the passage-way the man and Lloyd kept up their chat about bands and who was in and who was out and who had been up to what; he even gave Lloyd the exclusive on who was about to break up.

'I don't believe it!' Lloyd gushed. 'Wait 'til I tell them at school on Monday – they won't believe it either. It'll be the biggest break-up in the history of music!'

Monday seemed like a long, long way off. Like it might never come.

Sam shuffled along after Lloyd and Lloyd's new friend. He didn't have any other choice. He could have been completely wrong, of course, and Lloyd could be com-pletely right. He could wake up the next morning and discover that Green Day were downstairs and end up having breakfast with them, listen to them play all day, get their autographs and T-shirts emblazoned with their name and some CDs and other cool stuff, and then get driven home at the end of it. He'd tell Tab all about it first, and wouldn't she be just so jealous? She'd go the greenest green with envy.

And that's what Lloyd believed was going to happen.

He really did.

The man glanced back at Sam to make sure he was still following, and Sam knew – he felt it with a sharp stab of terror – that Lloyd was wrong. Terribly wrong.

He wished his friend would turn around. He wished he would stop blabbing on and on to the man. He wished he could say something that would make Lloyd realise what was happening, that they had to get away, that they had to escape. But Lloyd didn't turn around, not once. He'd forgotten all about his friend Sam.

Sam thought about making a dash for the front door by himself. If he could get away and raise the alarm, he could save Lloyd, so it wouldn't be like he had abandoned him or anything. He could hardly drag Lloyd, kicking and screaming, out of there; he wasn't strong enough for that. But the house was dark, and huge, and there were too many corridors and several staircases. They had just gone past another staircase. Sam couldn't do it alone. Besides, he remembered that the man had locked the front door after they had come in, and Sam could see the heavy clump of keys hanging off his smart black jeans. Jingle jangle, jingle jangle all the way to the bedrooms.

'Right, this is yours, Lloyd,' the man said. 'One of the best rooms in the house.'

'We can share a room,' Sam suggested quickly.

'No, not a good idea, and not fair on your mate, either,' he said to Sam. 'I mean, if you start feeling really unwell, I might have to call a doctor out for you, and then no one would get a decent night's kip.'

'Lloyd won't mind,' Sam said. 'Will you, Lloyd?'

Lloyd looked at him and shrugged. 'Doesn't make a difference to me.'

It does to me, Sam screamed inside his head, it does to me.

'Um, I'm not that good in big, old, dark houses,' Sam said with a nervous laugh. No one could ever accuse him of not trying his best. If this was a film, he'd have got an Oscar by now.

'Bit of a baby, are you, then? Never mind, diddums, I'll leave a night light on for you, and I'll even tuck you in if you like,' the man said, and he laughed with Lloyd.

'Yeah, grow up, Sam!' Lloyd said.

Sam could tell that Lloyd was annoyed with him for showing him up like that. *Lloyd annoyed with him* – Sam couldn't believe it. He wanted to take Lloyd by the shoulders and shake him until he saw what was in front of him.

'Please, Lloyd?' Sam's voice had shrunk to a whimper. He could tell it had worked though because Lloyd was looking sorry for him.

'Yeah, all right. If you must,' Lloyd said.

He'd said it reluctantly, but Sam knew that was for the man's benefit. Lloyd had seen sense at last. Well, not entirely, but once they were on their own, Sam would make sure that Lloyd knew what was going on, and then they could devise some kind of plan to get out.

'We can't have that now, Lloyd, can we? Don't worry about your friend. He'll be just fine. It'll do him good to grow up a bit just like you said. Anyway, I'm here to look out for both of you and that's what I'll do. You make yourself at home, Lloyd, and I'll be back to check you've got everything you need,' the man said pleasantly. 'Sam, you're just a bit further up here.' He walked on.

Sam looked back at Lloyd, hoping he could get a quick word with him while the man's back was turned, but Lloyd was gone. Sam couldn't believe it. Hadn't Lloyd been the one who'd said, 'Don't leave me on my own'?

And now he'd left Sam alone.

What had got into him?

At the end of the corridor the man stopped and opened the bedroom door. He reached in and switched the light on.

'In you go then, lad,' he said.

Sam stepped inside. It was a small, plain room with a neatly made bed, a bedside table with a little lamp, two chests of drawers and a big heavy wardrobe. There was no other furniture.

'There's a bathroom just through there.' The man indicated at a door half-hidden on the other side of the wardrobe. 'You'll find everything you need in there. Sleep tight now,' he said, and left the room.

Sam didn't really know what to do next. He surveyed the room again, and wondered whether it had ever been used before. It looked like the kind of room that the butler would have. Lloyd had been given the best room in the house, which probably meant it had a four-poster bed, or even a water bed, and other cool stuff.

Then Sam got annoyed with himself for thinking in that way because that was how Lloyd had been duped, made a complete idiot of, and Sam had almost fallen into the same way of thinking without even realising that was happening. He should think like Tab, his sister.

She always kept her cool; well, most of the time anyway, and didn't have to say, 'Use your brain, Sam, that's why it's in your head,' quite so much any more because Sam had learnt to use his brain a bit more. He'd had to, living with an older smart-arse sister, who knew everything about everything, and who had more common sense than practically everyone he knew, apart from his mum.

His dad didn't stand a chance in the common sense stakes, and as Tab was always saying, most men didn't, which wasn't entirely fair, but Sam had proved her wrong – until earlier that afternoon anyway.

He'd go to the loo and then decide what to do. Sam crossed the room to the bathroom, and then stopped suddenly in mid-stride. Jingle jangle, jingle jangle, and then the click of a key turning in the lock.

Sam swivelled round.

6

He was locked in. Again! Why? Well, it didn't take an A Level in Science to know the answer to that. Science was his worst subject, and it wasn't as though he didn't try — he did, and he wanted to be good at it, and that's what made it even worse. 'Just do your best,' his mum would say. But what if your best wasn't ever good enough?

Sam looked at the locked door, knowing that looking at it wasn't going to get it unlocked. Only a key would do that and he didn't have one. The man had it. Something hot prickled his eyes. It was the warning sign before the floodgates opened and he mutated into a snivelling baby, and he couldn't have that, not now. Not when there was so much to do.

Sam turned back round and went to the bathroom. It was as plain and sparse as the bedroom: a loo, a sink and a bathtub, soap and a towel. He splashed his face with ice-cold water from the tap, and the prickling in his eyes abated for a while, but then it started again and he couldn't control it this time. Within seconds, he was on his knees sobbing, blubbering, crying for his mum like he used to do when he was really little and had had a scary nightmare. He crawled out of the bathroom and curled up on the bed, burying his face in the pillow to the muffle the sound of his distress. Long minutes passed, it could have been hours, but Sam knew it wasn't. His watch said ten thirty when he checked it after the fountain had finally run dry. His pillow was soaked with tears. It was amazing how much water could come out of your eyes, and one day Sam would find out exactly how and why that happened, if he didn't almost fail his Science exam again that is.

He sat up on the bed, pulling the duvet out from under him, and huddled beneath it. The room had got colder. His eyes strayed to the locked door again, and he threw off the cover and jumped off the bed as a sudden thought struck him. If the man could lock him in, he might be able to lock the man out. *Might*, Sam thought, sizing up the chest of drawers. It was about his height and almost as long – and it was ancient looking, which meant it probably weighed an absolute ton. It was worth a go. 'Nothing ventured, nothing gained,' his dad, the king of clichés, always said. But what exactly would be gained by locking the man out? Actually, quite a lot, Sam thought.

He should be able to manage it: it couldn't be that heavy and he didn't have to carry it anywhere. All he had to do was slide it across the doorway. 'Easy peasy, lemon squeezey; no problemo; piece of piss,' Sam said loudly, enjoying each and every word with relish as his voice echoed round the empty room. He almost smiled to himself because in normal life he probably wouldn't say any of those things – and never out loud. But nothing was normal at the moment, and saying something out loud, even though it was a load of rubbish, didn't make him feel so wretched and alone. Actually having a project was pretty good. It would pass the time until help arrived. Although Sam didn't really think the cavalry were going to charge in and kill all the baddies because no one knew they were there. But surely the man would let them go in the morning? Sam was counting on it.

He set his feet a little bit apart and planted his hands on the chest of drawers, and then he pushed. It didn't move much. Okay, it was going to be tough, but Sam was well up for the job. He pushed harder, and the chest of drawers shifted a couple of inches. Hurrah, progress, but yes, it was going to take a while, he thought glumly, and he had no clue how much time he had before he had a visit from the man. 'Come on, Sam, put your back into it,' his mum cajoled. 'It's not that heavy. Oh, all right, I'll get Tab to give you a hand,' she would say in a resigned voice. His mum had a bad back so she couldn't lift heavy things, push furniture around, or even mow the lawn, and with his dad working long hours Sam was always called on to help out. He wished he did have Tab there to give him a hand: she was tough, and she never asked for help. The hot prickling sensation was coming back, but Sam couldn't let it win this time – he really had work to do.

He pushed again, and again, and again, and then he turned around and pressed his back into it, and slowly, slowly, agonisingly, painfully slowly, the chest of drawers inched its way across the wall. Sam kept pushing, his arms and legs going all soft and quivery, and it took all his strength to make them hard again, but he kept on pushing, and yelling, 'Put your back into it!' like his mum might have done if she was a yelling kind of person, which she wasn't, but if she could see him now, she would definitely be yelling it. Sam was sure of that.

Finally, it did reach the door, and a bit more pushing, and yelling, got it in front of the door. The door was well and truly blocked. No way anyone was coming in now. Sam fell to the floor in a heap, laughing breathlessly, and maybe a little hysterically, too.

He rolled over onto his back, where he stayed until he'd managed to stop the silly laughing, and get his breath back. He brought his wrist up to his face and his watch now said eleven. It had taken him half an hour to get the chest of drawers across the door! That was a ridiculously long time. Either he was much weaker than he thought, or the chest of drawers had been really, really heavy. Did that mean that the man wouldn't be able to get in? Of course it did. There was no way he could open the door into the room, so there was no way he could get in. The chest of drawers was a good height – it covered over half of the door. If the man got an axe and chopped his way in, he might have been able to get through the gap above the chest of drawers and the top of the door. But that only happened in films, Sam thought. So he was okay.

But, duh-brain, didn't that mean that he was stuck, too? Trapped? Forever? He stared up at the ceiling, thinking. And then he thought: *camera*. The man was probably doubled over having a laugh at the stupid kid with jelly arms and legs and tear-streaked face. Sam glanced around. No red dots, no glass eye watching silently. Phew, no camera. He wasn't being watched. He was alone, and he preferred it that way.

All alone by himself – the way Lloyd didn't want to be. Sam hoped he *was* all alone, like him. But Lloyd hadn't been locked in. The man had said he was going to check in on him, to make sure he had everything he needed. He hadn't done that for Sam. He'd shown him to his room and locked him in. What would Lloyd need, anyway? He was just going to go to sleep, like Sam, and when he woke up that famous band would be there and they were going to have a brilliant day. Weren't they?

Maybe the man just didn't like him, Sam thought, because he had been a bit of a baby, and that's why Lloyd was getting better treatment. Lloyd had been cool, and friendly, and Lloyd's dad was high up in the music business, so the man had to be much nicer to him than to Sam.

But it all kept going round in circles in Sam's head. Round and round like a crazy carousel with no brakes. 'Come on, Sam, focus. Keep your eye on the ball.'

He heard water running. He must have left the tap on in the bathroom. It was funny that he'd only noticed it now – it must have been running for an hour. He was just getting off the floor when somewhere, not too far away, he heard a door slam shut. He bolted towards the bedroom light switch and flicked it off and then ran into the bathroom and in one swift move turned the tap off and the bathroom light on. He left the door slightly ajar so he had some light in the bedroom, but nothing that could be seen through the cracks. He took the bedside table and placed it next to the chest of drawers and climbed up. For a moment all he could hear was the thudding of his heart. *Baboom, baboom, baboom, baboom.*

Sam knew it was beating too fast, but how do you slow it down? Breathing might help, he thought. So that's what he did. He breathed in and out slowly a couple of times, and then couldn't wait any longer and pressed his ear to the door. The babooming had quietened down a bit, or at least it wasn't pounding in his head as much. But from the rest of the house all he heard was silence. He listened harder.

Or were there some sounds? Could he hear some music? Voices? Laughter? Maybe the band had arrived and Lloyd was having a ball with them. Or maybe the music and laughter were all inside Sam's head. He couldn't work it out. He suddenly felt exhausted. Too tired to think. He should try and get some sleep. Things always looked better in the morning, at least that's what his mum always promised, and most of the time it was true. But not always.

He clambered back down off the chest of drawers and picked up the bedside table to put it back where it came from. Click, click, click, click. Sam knew instantly what it was and he almost jumped out of his skin. A key was turning in the lock. He dropped the table, but it didn't make any noise on the carpet and it had saved Sam from screaming the house down like that girl had done in that scary film they had watched in the car. The door didn't open, but the key was turned in the lock again, and again. Click, click, click, click. Someone was trying to get in and thought the key wasn't working properly. It wouldn't take them long to work out that the key was fine, and that it was the door that wasn't opening.

Ha! Take that, you creep! Sam thought, but his elation was short lived.

It hadn't taken the man long to realise what was going on. Sam heard a yell, and this time it wasn't an imaginary sound, it was horribly real, and it meant one thing: the man was angry, very angry. Sam inched back towards the bathroom door. A violent shove jarred against the chest of drawers, but it didn't budge, not an inch. Another loud slam. The man must have put his shoulder to the door that time and the chest of drawers shuddered in response. It didn't look as though it had moved, but Sam couldn't be sure. He took another step back as another slam battered the chest of drawers. This time he saw it move, but not much, just a tiny fraction. Sam cringed, waiting for the next slam. Nothing happened. There was that silence again.

Back-up plan, Sam hissed at himself. You need a back-up plan in case he gets in. The problem was Sam couldn't think of anything. His brain had gone on strike or something because he kept trying to think, and all he could see was the chest of drawers lying on its side and the bedroom door wide open. Focus, Sam. Focus. But Sam couldn't focus. His dad's voice began to fade and Sam couldn't work out why. Help, Dad. Please help me. Please come. I need you. Please, Dad, come now. Please – the words tumbled helter-skelter through his mind as the tears toppled down his face. Sam knew his dad couldn't help him.

Slam. Slam. The man was back. He wasn't going to stop until he was inside the room and this time it didn't sound as though he was using his shoulder. He was using something big and heavy to pulverize the door. It was some kind of sledge hammer or battering ram, or maybe even an axe. Sam began to sob. He backed up, right up to the bathroom doorway, and listened to the steady beat of the *slam, slam*. What would he do when the man came in? *Slam, slam*. What would he do when the man came in? *Slam, slam*. What would he do when the man came in?

Part of Sam's brain must have been working because it came up with an answer. He would overpower him and kill him if he came anywhere near him. Oh really, Sam. How are you going to do that?

A weapon, that's what he needed. Now he was in a frenzy. The man could break through at any minute and Sam had no weapon. He searched round wildly for something to use, anything. He rummaged through the chest of drawers, but all the drawers were empty. The wardrobe had a couple of moth-eaten coats hanging in it and nothing else. The bedside table was the only thing left, and that wasn't a very practical weapon to wield. The only thing he could do with it was chuck it at the man and then try and run past him. He would have to aim for his head, try and knock him out or something. No, that wouldn't work. The man would just swat it away with one hand. Maybe he could hide it behind his back until the man was close, then he could swing it out from behind him and crack it across the man's head.

Get real, you stupid idiot, he told himself harshly. This wasn't an action movie where the kids all had stunt doubles, and never actually lifted a finger, never mind wield real weapons. This was real life, and the worst nightmare of Sam's life.

7

The man must have taken a breather because the slam, slam stopped for a while. Sam started thinking again, and the tears dried up. It was much easier to think without that racket going on. Okay, no weapon apart from the bedside table. Then he remembered his rucksack. Maybe there was something in there he could use. But where was it? He looked round the room, trying to think back to when he'd had it last. He had taken it out of the car with him and then they had gone straight to the games room. So that's where it must be, exactly where it was of no use to anyone.

There was probably nothing much in there anyway, Sam thought. A pocket dictionary would have been useless. There was his school homework, and considering the circumstances Sam thought his mum would probably write him a note explaining why he hadn't been able to do it. It would go something like, 'My son, Samuel Parker, could not do his homework because he and his new friend, Lloyd, were kidnapped on Friday by a demented madman, and locked up in a room.'

And that was pretty much all there was in his rucksack, oh, apart from his pencil case – his pencil case which contained a compass with a very shiny, sharp point. Now *that* would have come in very handy. But it was way down the corridor, past his blockaded door and the madman, and there was no way Sam was going out that way.

The slamming began again in earnest, setting Sam's heart pounding. He couldn't bear it any longer. He backed up right into the bathroom and closed the door. It muffled the sound a bit, but not enough. Then he noticed the key in the lock, and wondered why he hadn't seen it earlier. He locked the door. One more obstacle for the man to get through before he got to him.

Sam sat down on the edge of the bath; his legs had gone all wobblyish again and his hands were shaking. What he needed was a mobile phone. He wished he'd asked his parents for one for his last birthday, although he knew he probably wouldn't have got one then. Tab had only got hers last year and she was three years older than him. It was only for emergencies, but she was always texting her friends on it and there was never an emergency in sight. Lots more kids his age had them now and not *all* of them got mugged. He'd said that to his dad just a few days ago, but it hadn't cut much ice with him. He thought it might now though.

He looked around the bathroom just to make sure he hadn't missed anything like a razor blade or something else that could be used as a weapon. There was a loo brush, but Sam didn't think that was going to hold the man at bay for long. There were a couple of manky old bathrobes hanging behind the door, which were completely useless. And then he saw something better than a weapon. Something he must have been blind not to have noticed.

An escape route. A window.

It was small, above the sink, but Sam knew he could wriggle through it. He was only a skinny kid, wasn't he? No problem. He was getting out, and he smiled despite the fact that as he thought of escape and getting home, he realised that he was one floor up, and that Lloyd was still trapped somewhere in the house.

Sam clambered onto the edge of the sink, placing his feet on either side of the taps to balance himself, and lifted the handle and pushed. It must have been stuck because it didn't open straight away. There were cobwebs, which Sam didn't mind because he liked spiders, and a thick layer of dust on the panes, which meant it hadn't been used in a long time. He had to whack it open and that was okay because the man was making enough racket to hide any noise that Sam made. He slammed the heel of his palm into it, swapping hands after several blows as his hands began to sting and then throb with pain. Why couldn't it have just opened? Why was everything so hard? Sam cried. Tears ran down his face, but he didn't bother trying to control them. He knew they would stop eventually.

He had to keep stopping and checking that the man hadn't got through the bedroom door, which held him up because the window was still jammed shut and hadn't budged an inch. But with every slam from beyond the bathroom door, Sam knew the man was getting closer and closer.

Sam went frantic and pummelled the window with both hands, screaming and crying at the same time. He wasn't even aware of the noise he was making any more. He didn't care; he just had to get out. A final flurry of blows and the window shot open without warning, just as the bathroom door juddered with a sickening thump.

And then silence.

The man was on the other side of the bathroom door. When had he got through the bedroom door? Sam didn't know. He didn't know how long he'd been standing outside listening to him screaming and crying. Sam held his breath, and waited for the man to speak through the door. It wouldn't be long, he thought. He was right – it wasn't.

'I know you're in there, you silly boy. Come on now, open the door,' the man said. He said it very nicely, which wasn't what Sam was expecting at all. It would have been less freaky if he'd yelled and shouted at him.

'It would save us both a lot of trouble if you just open the door, Sam,' and again it was said in that cloyingly nice and pleasant tone that made Sam's skin crawl.

But Sam said nothing and he did nothing. He wasn't falling for that, and did the bloke really think he would be stupid enough to open the door?

'Come on, Sam. Open the door and I'll explain the whole thing to you. Man to man.'

Sam remained silent. As far as he was concerned nothing needed explaining. Sam was tempted to put his hands over his ears, but he needed to hear what the man was saying, too. It could all have been a silly misunderstanding, couldn't it?

The man continued, 'Lloyd's not feeling too good, Sam. He's been asking for you,' the man said. 'You're not going to let him down are you?'

Lloyd, why didn't you listen to me? Sam thought angrily, and then he felt really bad. It wasn't as though any of this was Lloyd's fault.

'I don't know what you're so afraid of, lad, but you're going to have to come out of there sometime. Lloyd's really not well. I've had to call the doctor out for him. Go and sit with Lloyd while I go down and wait by the front door for the doctor. He'll be here soon.'

Sam didn't believe him for a minute, although the bloke was good and Sam had to give him that. He was so convincing that just for a tiny split second, Sam almost thought about opening the door and going to Lloyd. He wanted to be with his friend. He was fed up with being on his own. But what good would that do any of them? No, the best way to help Lloyd was to get away and come back with help. Lots of it.

Sam stuck his head out of the window and peered into the darkness. It was pitch black and he couldn't see a thing. In the background the man's voice droned on in its softly persuasive tone. Sam kept looking out of the window until his eyes adjusted to the darkness. Now he could make out the outline of trees beyond the house, and between them an expanse of lawn dotted with shrubs and bushes.

Then he looked directly down at the drop.

Okay, it wasn't going to be easy, but it was doable. It was better than the alternative. So what was he waiting for? He looked at the drop again. It didn't look so bad, plus at the bottom there was some grass and bushes that would break his fall. He gripped both sides of the window and hoisted himself up so he was crouching on the narrow ledge. He looked down again, hesitating. He glanced back towards the bathroom door.

The man was still talking, but the nicey-nice tone had gone and been replaced with extreme annoyance verging on anger.

'Don't be stupid and open the door now!'

Sam had no intention of being stupid enough for that.

'No one's going to hurt you.' The kick that whacked the door told Sam that that was a complete lie.

The threats would start next, Sam thought, and as if the man had heard him his next words proved Sam right.

'If I have to break the door down, it'll be worse for you. There's no way out that way, you know.'

And that's where you're wrong, Sam whispered softly.

There *was* a way out, and Sam was going to take it. All he needed was a rope or something. It didn't have to reach all the way to the ground, just long enough for him to dangle off and then the drop wouldn't be so bad. He noticed the bathrobes had fallen off the peg and were lying in a heap on the floor. They still had their cord threaded through the loops.

Unbelievable. Finally something had gone his way.

Sam was off the window ledge in seconds. He pulled the cords out from their loops and ran his fingers down their length. They looked strong enough to bear his weight, but could have done with being several feet longer, even when they were tied together. They were better than nothing; better than the alternative. He knotted them together securely with a triple knot, and then tied one end of it to a tap, his fingers fumbling with the knot. This bit had to be done right otherwise he didn't stand a chance. He started again and made a better job of it. No way was it going to come off that tap, ever. Sam threw the other end of the window and climbed back up onto the ledge. He peered down and saw it swaying in the light breeze. It could have done with being a bit thicker too, Sam thought. But it was still better than nothing.

Okay this was the tricky part. He had to get his legs out of the window first and try and wrap them round the cord. He manoeuvred his body round so that he was facing into the bathroom, and swung his legs out one by one, still keeping a tight grip on the window frame. Now he was dangling in open air, half in and half out of the window, and the problem was he couldn't see the dangling cord now because his legs were in the way. He swung his legs around a bit, hoping one of them would catch the cord, but he couldn't tell whether he had managed it. Okay, forget that part, he told himself. He would have to climb down, hand over hand instead. He had to let go with his right hand and take hold of the cord, but his fingers were reluctant to loosen their grip on the sturdy window frame. The cord wasn't too far to reach – it was right next to his hand, but he still couldn't let go of the frame.

Why did the cord look so flimsy all of a sudden, and what if he hadn't tied the knot properly? What if it gave way?

The bathroom door shuddered under the impact of a violent blow. The man had finally lost patience. It wouldn't take him long to get through the bathroom door now because it wasn't as solid as the bedroom door had been. Sam reached for the cord. If it gave way he would have to remember to roll as soon as he hit the ground. That's what skydivers and parachutists did, and, apparently, kids who jumped out of bathroom windows. Whatever happened he would have to leg it into the trees as fast as he could, because it wouldn't take the man long to get downstairs and out of the house after him.

Another heavy blow at the door jolted any thoughts of what he had to do when he landed right out of his head. He took a deep breath and closed his eyes.

And then he jumped.

8

He swung out off the window ledge, his hands sliding down the cord, falling, slipping almost before he could get a good strong grip on it with his legs swinging free in the air. This was how it felt when he was diving into a pool, his legs cycling the air and his hands above his head in total abandon, laughing, heading for the big splash when he would hit the water, his friends on the diving board watching or larking about in the water waiting for him. Except there was no water below him, and no friends larking about.

He had to slow down, get a better grip on the cord and get his feet up against the wall before he slipped any further. He knew the theory. He had seen people abseiling down sheer cliffs and over the sides of tall buildings on TV – they had made it look so easy. But they usually had the advantage of safety harnesses and years of training and stuff, and Sam hadn't got any of those things. It was just him and the cord of some tatty old bathrobes, and if you considered that then he wasn't doing such a bad job. At least he wasn't afraid of heights because if he was he would be cowering in the corner of the bathroom listening to the man beating the door down instead of being a few minutes away from making good his escape.

He focussed his mind on climbing down the length of the cord and didn't notice the head sticking out of the window, watching him. When he glanced up, he panicked. His hand under hand technique on the cord went out of the window and he started slipping down too fast again. His feet lost their grip on the wall and scrambled madly through empty air, which must have made the cord start swinging to and fro and gather speed. Sam made his legs go still, but he couldn't control the momentum of the cord. It swung him way out and then back towards the wall and Sam couldn't stop it. He screamed as he went slamming into the wall with a sickening crunch.

The breath was knocked out of him and his whole side felt battered and bruised, but somehow he had managed to keep his grip on the cord. He looked up. The man was leering down at him; in his hands he held the cord.

'Hold tight,' he called down. 'This might hurt a bit!'

He swung Sam out again and there was nothing Sam could do about it except scream, and scream he did, as loud and for as long as he could. Surely someone would hear him. Maybe Lloyd would hear his friend in trouble and come rushing down to his rescue? No, Lloyd wasn't coming to his rescue; Lloyd wasn't feeling well. Remember? But why wasn't he feeling well? What was wrong with him? Was *he* getting *his* head smashed in? Crunch. Sam hit the wall again, but this time he'd got his leg out first, which lessened the impact a bit, but still knocked the breath out of him. He had to jump the rest of the way. He knew he did. Don't look down, he told himself, don't look down. Just do it.

But he did look down, and it was still a long way to the bottom. There were paving slabs that ran all the way round the house, which he hadn't noticed before. If he fell on them he'd crack his head open. He had to time it right.

'Ready for some more?' the man asked.

Sam knew it wasn't a question. The cord started swinging him to and fro, gaining momentum for a bigger impact against the wall. The man really didn't like him. He swung him in and out, in and out. The next one, Sam decided, the next one was the one. It would bring him out beyond the paving slabs, so that he landed in the bushes or on the grass.

Okay, Sam, get ready, he whispered to himself. This was it; this was the one. He counted one, two, three in his head and then let go of the cord.

'Aaaaagh!' he screamed, all the way down.

He plummeted, his arms flapping the air uselessly, and tumbled into a bush. He rolled as soon as he hit the bush, but ended up getting more and more entwined in its foliage, falling deeper into its heart. Clothes ripped, scratched, and bleeding, but alive and with no broken bones, he scrambled through the choking density of branches and leaves until he found a way out. But he didn't crawl out into the open, not yet. He lay very, very still and peered through the bush instead, his eyes searching for the bathroom window. He found it. The man was still holding the cord and looking down intently at the bush, scrutinising it. Sam stayed motionless, barely daring to breathe, waiting. Long moments passed until finally the man started pulling the cord up, back into the bathroom. The window closed with a bang. Sam crawled out of the bush, and ran for his life.

He had no more than a couple of minutes to reach the trees, he guessed. It would take the man that long to get downstairs and find the right keys for the front door – plus he wouldn't know which way Sam had gone. The problem was that Sam couldn't work out quite where he was in relation to the front door. He needed to get his bearings right so he didn't get lost, but he had to get away quickly, too. He hazarded a guess that he was somewhere to the west of the front door. He belted across the springy, well-tended lawn, heading east, towards the trees, and then changed his mind and went directly towards the dark safety of the woods just in case the man got out of the house faster than Sam had estimated he would and spotted him.

In his head he saw an image of the man running through the corridor, pelting down the stairs three at a time, with the keys going jingle jangle, the right key ready in his hand to unlock the door. It was enough to spur Sam on, and he put on a mad burst of speed, grimacing at the intense pain in his side, but he didn't let it slow him down. Almost there, almost there, and then he collapsed in a heap behind the first tree. He wriggled round, keeping his head down, and looked back across the lawn. Someone had switched the outside lights on and Sam could see the outline of the whole house clearly.

His room hadn't been on the west side of the house, it was more like at the back. Now he had his bearings, he had to decide what to do next: head round to the front of the house and from there make his way down the drive towards the gate, or head deeper into the woods and find a house or a main road from there. He lay sprawled flat against the wet, muddy ground trying to decide. He knew he was wasting time, but his heart was pounding so loud it wouldn't let his brain work. He had to wait for the pounding to slow down and for his brain to start working or he might end up doing the wrong thing – which might get him caught.

Think, idiot brain, *think*. What should he do? Where should he go? There were pros and cons to both directions. If he went round the front there was a chance he might get spotted, and also that was probably what the man expected him to do. But if he got to the gate then he was almost at the road and all he had to do was follow it until he could flag down a passing car, or the road might lead to a bigger road, or a village, or something, anything.

The other option of heading into the woods was bound to be safer. No way the man would spot him in this much darkness and he would definitely get away. But he might get lost, lose his bearings, go round and round in circles alone in the dark. But he wouldn't get caught.

Out of the corner of his eye, he saw movement. He slithered right up to the edge of the line of trees to get a better look. The man had rounded the side of the house and was heading directly for the patch of ground below the bathroom window. Sam held his breath. Somewhere behind him an owl hooted and Sam ducked down as the man's gaze travelled towards the woods. The owl hooted twice more, went silent and hooted again. It could have been saying, *he's here, he's here*, and although Sam knew that it wasn't, he just wished the owl would shut up because the man kept looking into the trees every time it hooted. It must have got Sam's message because six hoots later the bird fell silent and didn't speak again. The man continued along the back of the house and Sam breathed more easily.

He didn't seem to be in much of a hurry to get there because he walked slowly, which was a bit odd until Sam realised that he probably thought the fall had killed Sam, and dead kids didn't get up and run away. Well, he was in for a surprise then, because this kid *had* run away.

But what about Lloyd? What about Lloyd, Sam thought angrily. He had abandoned Sam first, and anyway, Sam wasn't abandoning him. He was going to get help.

At the bushes the man halted and with a sudden movement, which Sam hadn't been expecting at all, he swung the stick he had been carrying at his side into the bushes. Sam winced involuntarily and covered his face with his hands as the man lifted the hefty stick over his head and brought it crashing down on the bushes again, and again. He gave them a good thrashing, beating and tearing them aside, searching. He threw the stick aside and got down on his hands and knees to look under the canopy of branches and leaves.

Sam didn't need to watch any more. He had to get away. He wriggled backwards ever so slowly, flat on his stomach, and didn't stand up until he was deep inside the enveloping darkness of the woodland.

9

Inside the heart of silent darkness nothing stirred. Sam crouched in the hollow of a tree, waiting, thinking. He had expected the man to come into the woods after him, but he hadn't yet, and Sam wondered why. Maybe he was waiting at the edge of the woods for him to come out because he knew it was only a matter of time before Sam came out screaming when the dark woods got to him. Most kids were scared of being by themselves in dark, lonely woods, and Sam was no different. Or maybe the man was creeping through the woods looking for him and Sam just couldn't hear him because he was an expert at creeping. There were people, real people who could do that, and not just characters in books like *Lord of the Rings* where Aragorn could travel through woods and forests and never make a sound, never leave a footprint. Aragorn could track people, hobbits, orcs, basically anything that moved, but somehow Sam didn't think that this man could do any of those things because if he could, he'd have been here by now.

Sam tried hard not to look at the marks he had left on the ground. His backwards belly wriggle had made a little furrow that extended from the edge of the woods almost to where Sam was hunkered down. You didn't need to be an expert tracker to follow those tracks. He might as well have got up and yelled, 'Here I am! Come and get me.'

Maybe the man was afraid of the dark woods and that's why he hadn't followed Sam in, but that seemed an unlikely explanation even to Sam. Grown-ups weren't afraid of the dark, and neither was Sam, usually. This was different. This was a different kind of darkness.

He should get going before it got too late. He checked his watch; it was just after one, which meant it was highly unlikely he'd be able to flag down a passing car, or bump into someone walking their dog. Who'd walk their dog at one o'clock in the morning? Only a nutter, and Sam had had enough of nutters. The thing was he still had to get out of the woods.

Was it safe to move now, or should he wait a bit longer? The man could be hiding behind one of the trees waiting for Sam to make a move, and then Sam would really be stuffed, but on the other hand if he lay there for much longer he'd lose his advantage. The trouble was Sam couldn't get up, even though the ground beneath him was cold and damp and his toes had gone numb, even though it was pitch black all around, even though the man was nowhere in sight. He just couldn't get up.

He knew he couldn't stay there; he had to get moving. But he was scared, even more scared than he had been in the house, which didn't make any sense to him. He wasn't trapped in a locked room any more. He was free. He had escaped. Yes, him, Sam Parker, not exactly famous for his daring deeds or physical prowess, had escaped! So why was he stuck now? Woods were just trees, a collection of trees, and it was dark because the sun was round the other side of the world. In fact he should feel grateful for the dark because it meant it would be a lot harder for the man to find him.

Logic wasn't working for Sam; he was still afraid. He knew what he had to do. He had to pretend he wasn't Sam any more. He had to be somebody else. Someone who wasn't afraid of anything. He wasn't very good at acting and he'd never had a leading part in a school play yet, but this wasn't like acting, and it wasn't a school play. He had to think of a character he'd like to be and then pretend he was him. Someone clever, and fearless. He chose someone.

Sam looked back towards the direction in which the house lay one last time. Time to get the hell out of there. Okay, so if the house was that way, then it stood to reason that out of the woods had to be the other way. The next tree along wasn't too far off: four or five long strides at the most. Sam took a deep breath and turned and ran for it. Halfway there he thought he heard something behind him, something which sounded like heavy footsteps following, and he began to turn his head, a scream rising in his throat, the blood pounding in his ears. No one there, Sam thought, relieved, and he was almost at the safety of the next tree. Then his foot caught on a protruding tree root and he went down heavily. Tears sprang to his eyes. Idiot, idiot, idiot, he sobbed as he lay sprawled, his face in the wet, muddy ground. This had never happened to Alex Rider, the most fearless teenage secret agent the world had ever known.

Sam got up carefully, wincing at the shooting pain, and wondered whether he'd broken his ankle. He put his weight on it gingerly, testing it out before he attempted to walk on it. There was pain, but it wasn't unbearable, therefore it couldn't be broken. He hobbled towards the tree and pressed his back up against it, its solid weight reassuringly comforting, and waited. There was nothing, not a sound. He glanced back just to make sure, but the coast was clear. He limped across to the next tree and hid behind it. Tree by tree he made his way through the woods, knowing that he was losing time by doing it that way, but he couldn't do it any other way. Each tree-stop added a minute while he got his breath back and could hear again and check that he was still alone. It should have got easier the further away he went from the house, but it didn't, and maybe that was because the trees weren't spaced that far apart and so Sam knew he wasn't actually getting very far very quickly. There had been no sign of the man, though. Sam thought he must have given up on him and gone back to the house. Or that's what he was hoping anyway.

Then the trees stopped suddenly. He had reached the edge of the woods. Sam stood still and looked out. The moon peeped through the thick clouds teasing him with a glimpse of the countryside beyond. He could make out fields and more trees, but no road, no houses, and no people. He would have run across those open fields without stopping, without looking back, but he couldn't. He was trapped. A really high fence stood in the way. How the on earth was he going to get over a fence that high?

He curled his fingers round the cold metal bars, his knuckles glowing ghostly white as he pushed and pulled, hoping they would budge, but they didn't, not one millimetre. Tears of rage at the madman who had designed this fence pricked his eyes and spilled on to his hands still clutching futilely at the metal bars. The bars were wrought iron, rock solid, built to last, built to keep intruders out. He blinked the tears away and looked up. He was pretty good at climbing trees, but he knew he wouldn't be able to climb this fence.

It must have been about twenty feet high with a roll of barbed wire running along the top, so even if he managed to shin up the bars, which was impossible, he'd be cut to shreds trying to get over the top, or end up skewered on the spikes each iron railing was topped with.

He couldn't squeeze out of his nightmare through the bars either. If he were three years old he might have had a chance of getting through, but they were set too close together for an eleven-year-old. He could squeeze his leg through up to his thigh, but that was about it and no use at all.

He couldn't go over the top of the fence. And he couldn't go through it. He turned his attention to the bottom of the fence. Every tenth railing looked to be anchored on a post set deep in the ground with a horizontal bar running about half a foot off the ground linking the whole maddening, terrifyingly solid structure. He'd never be able to squirm through the gap between the bar and the ground – it couldn't have been more than three or four inches wide. He got down on his belly and tested it just in case. No way. Not a chance. He stood up and moved further along to a different section of fencing. It was exactly the same. Whoever had paid for it had got their moneys' worth.

Now what was he supposed to do?

He could have sat down and cried, the old Sam would have, but that's not what the new Sam did. He felt strangely calm, strangely focussed. He didn't feel like him any more, maybe that was why.

The only thing left to do was to follow the fence around the property and hope for a loose bar, or a bigger gap to squeeze through or under. There had to be one. He became aware of his ankle throbbing dully. He hunted around for a decent-sized stick, something he could use as a weapon as well as to help support his dodgy ankle. When he found one he began his limp-walk along the wrought-iron fence, and ended up running the stick across the bars as he went. The fence seemed to go on for miles without a break, without one single loose bar. On the other side of it were open fields, woods, or overgrown hedges and bushes that you couldn't see a thing through.

Sam had got so used to the quiet that when the owl started hooting again he almost jumped out of his skin. Sam didn't know much about owls, or why they hooted when they did, but now he wished he did. Was it a warning? Did they hoot when they felt threatened, or were they calling to warn other owls of danger?

He used the cover of a tree to scan the area, but it was hard to see anything deep in the woods where all the moonlight did was cast menacing shadows. He had to carry on. Reluctantly, he left the safety of the tree and went back to following the fence. The trees thinned out and when they eventually came to an end Sam knew he was near the gate. He hunched over, making himself small, and crept out towards it. It was closed, as he knew it would be, but he thought he might be able to climb it. As he approached it he knew he had thought wrong. Somehow he hadn't remembered it being as high as that. He gave it a shake, but like the rest of the fence it didn't give an inch. He ran across to the other side of it and squatted in the undergrowth.

There were a couple of options open to him now. He could wait there until someone came, or left, and try and sneak through while the gate was open. The only problem with that was that it was now one thirty and there was no one likely to arrive, or leave for that matter. There was probably a whole army of gardeners and cleaners for a place like this, but they wouldn't be arriving in the dead of night, and tomorrow was Saturday. No one worked on a Saturday.

He looked back across the driveway to where he had just come from, trying to figure out what to do next. He knew he couldn't hide out until Monday morning, and if the rest of the fence was anything like the other side, then there was no way out. There was no grand escape. There was no way he could get help for Lloyd. There was no hope.

And then it got worse.

'Sam!'

It came from the other side of the driveway, still quite far away, but too close. Sam turned and fled into the woods. He stumbled along blindly, trying to put as much distance between him and the voice as possible. Then he stopped. Think, Sam, think of a plan. He had to do something. Something clever. He ripped off the cuff of his shirtsleeve and headed back, only slowing down as he approached the gate. He caught a brief glimpse of the light of a torch as it swept a wide arc through the woods on the other side. He still had a little time left. He flung the cuff through the bars of the gate and ran for the trees. This time he didn't head deep into the woods. He followed the line of trees up the driveway, running as fast as he could. His ankle screamed with pain, but he ignored it. He didn't have much time.

The trees rounded with the bend in the driveway and then petered out within sight of the house. The outside lights were still on and lit up the vast expanse of lawn between Sam and the house. I can do it, Sam said to himself, I can do it. It wasn't that vast; he'd be across it in a flash. The man wouldn't see him because he was still down by the gate. Still Sam hesitated, unsure, glancing back down the drive and up towards the house. Was this being clever? Or was this the most stupidest thing he had done? The thing was he had run out of ideas. He could have gone round and round in circles, but the man knew the land better than him, and Lloyd was trapped inside the house. Sam couldn't get him any help. He was Lloyd's only help. This was his only chance to get Lloyd out. He had to go back for him – plus the man would never guess that Sam would go back to the house.

Then Sam thought of something that hadn't occurred to him at all. What if Lloyd was already dead? Don't be stupid, you moron, he hissed at himself. Lloyd wasn't dead. He couldn't be dead. He was – he was ill, or something, but not dead. Definitely not dead. Sam started shivering. He had to get in the house and get Lloyd out before it was too late. Sam just wished he could stop shaking. He would go as soon as he did. It wasn't cold, or if it was it wasn't the cold that Sam felt. Breathing in deeply wasn't helping either. His hands had gone clammy and cold under their coating of mud. He clutched the stick hard with both hands to steady himself. He was running out of time. It had to be now.

He glanced back down the driveway towards the gate one last time and began the count.

One, two, three, GO!

He ran faster than he had ever run before, but the grass seemed to extend on further and further as he ran, and then he was past it. Within seconds he was across the gravel drive and at the front door. It stood wide open. The shiny, white flash car was still parked outside, but Sam barely glanced at it. The front door beckoned, and, for the second time that night, Sam entered the house.

10

Sam went past the gilded mirrors and the dusty portraits of the oldies, and it felt like a lifetime ago that he had been there last. But it hadn't been months, or weeks, or days, it had just been a few hours ago. He took the stairs two at a time, barely noticing the pain in his ankle. He was focussed again; intent on finding his friend and then getting as far away as possible. Sam knew there wasn't much time.

He got to the first floor and stopped to make sure he had his bearings right. The house was full of staircases; well, at least three that Sam could remember passing. What would have been useful was one of those state-of-the-art new watches that had a built-in compass; he could have made good use of it today. Soon they'd make one which had a mobile phone built into it too, and when they did he was going to get one no matter how much it cost. He wasn't even going to bother begging and pleading for it; he'd get a Saturday job and pay for it himself. He would have done anything for a mobile phone right now – even killed for it. If Lloyd had remembered to charge his stupid phone they wouldn't be in this mess now. Sam would get a mobile that had a solar battery built into it.

Phone! Land line! Why hadn't he thought of that before? There had to be one somewhere in this place. But first he had to find Lloyd. Or should he find a phone? Sam hesitated at the top of the stairs, uncertain. No, it had to be Lloyd first, before the man came back, and finding a phone would be faster with two of them looking.

He ran down the corridor opening every door on either side of it. None of them were locked. At the far end of the corridor, he found the games room and reached inside and grabbed his coat and their rucksacks from where they lay leaning against the wall. They had dumped them there as soon as they'd entered and beheld the land of dreams; the biggest and best array of games ever brought together in one room. Sam felt sick at the sight of them. He didn't think he would want to play one of those games ever again. He stuffed his coat into his rucksack, swung it over his back, picked up Lloyd's rucksack, and left the room.

He followed the corridor until it got to the point where it branched in two directions and this time he didn't pause. Their rooms were off to the right, he was sure of it. He went swiftly past the third staircase, knowing he was close. Lloyd's room was first. He couldn't remember the exact door, but it didn't matter. He'd find it. Further down the passage there was an open door, the light blazing from within, and Sam shuddered. The remains of his door were lying in a thousand bits of splintered fragments on the floor outside. He had been lucky. It could have been him.

He went more slowly now, but opened all the doors on both sides of the corridor. He couldn't remember why he'd decided to do that any more, but it had seemed like a good idea at the time. Someone must have done it in a book he'd read and it had made sense.

He knew when he got there that it was Lloyd's room. It was the only other one apart from his that had an open door. The door stood ajar, which was good, but odd because it should have been locked. Sam hadn't even thought about what he would do next if it had been locked. He wondered why the man hadn't bothered to lock Lloyd in. Maybe he had been in too much of a hurry to get outside and see what had become of his other prisoner.

Sam glanced back the way he had come. The corridor was empty, but Sam didn't know how much time he had. If the man didn't spot the ripped-off cuff that he'd thrown outside the gate, then he'd probably continue his circuit of the perimeter fence. If he did spot it, he'd go after Sam down the bumpy track towards the road. Either way it meant that there should be tons of time to get Lloyd out, find a phone, and then hide until help arrived.

Sam pushed the door open and stepped inside Lloyd's room. He placed Lloyd's rucksack on the floor to keep both his hands free. The room was dimly lit by a soft lamp and it wasn't a bedroom. There were a couple of sofas piled high with cushions, a shiny glass coffee table, a big flat-screen TV, a camcorder set up on a tripod, a stereo system, but no cameras up in the corners of the room, and no Lloyd. There were two doors at the far end of the room on either side of the window. One would lead to the bathroom, Sam thought, and the other one to the bedroom, which would probably be locked and that was why the outer door had been open. What would he do if it was locked though? Break the door down? Kick it in? Get real, duh-brain, you know there's no way you've got enough strength for that, he told himself. It was possible the man had left the bunch of keys lying around somewhere. Sam should have looked for it on his way up, but no – that would have wasted too much time and, besides, the man probably had them in his pocket, or they were hanging off his trendy black jeans.

Sam tried the door to the left of the window first. It wasn't locked, but one look inside told him it was the bathroom, a very plush one full of knick-knacks and stuff and nothing like Sam's bathroom. Sam checked for cameras and a window. No cameras, but a nice big window. There were two large white fluffy bathrobes hanging off shiny chrome pegs, and Sam took the ties from both of them and stuffed them quickly into his rucksack. He took a bar of soap and a towel, and then spotted a large, heavy glass paperweight, like a marble which had had a serious dose of steroids. Not an ideal weapon, but a whack over the head with that would knock someone out for sure. It was solid and heavier than it looked, but it just about fit into Sam's fist. He put it in his pocket, within hand-reach.

He stepped out of the bathroom and crossed the room. Lloyd had to be in this room, behind that door. But was it locked or was it open? Sam reached for the handle but hesitated for a moment. He might find Lloyd fast asleep, oblivious to everything that happened, or waiting for the man to come and tell him that the mythical pop group had arrived. Maybe it was just Sam that the man had it in for. Or the door might be locked and then what would he do?

The thoughts tumbled through his head as he hesitated, and he knew he was wasting time again. But he was scared. He wanted Lloyd to be all right. He gripped the handle with shaking fingers and turned it. The door swung inwards, moaning gently on its hinges.

It was dark inside and at first Sam couldn't see a thing. He put his hand out for the light switch and then thought better of it. A light being switched on might alert the man. He could think it was Lloyd, but Sam didn't want to take the risk. He waited a minute while his eyes adjusted to the darkness and when they did Sam saw that the room was huge and packed with large pieces of furniture, their silhouettes standing to attention like sentries on duty.

He did a quick check for cameras and an escape route; it had become second nature to him now. There was a large window to his left, veiled with a wispy net curtain that filtered the moonlight into the room, but the drapes were still tied back. No cameras in the top corners of the room. At the centre of the room was a king-size bed, tussled sheets covered it with pillows at odd angles. The duvet lay in a heap on the floor. The bed was empty, and there was no sign of Lloyd.

'Lloyd. Lloyd,' Sam whispered. There were too many dark recesses, too many odd-shaped shadows. Lloyd could have been hiding in any of them.

Sam crept round the room softly, listening carefully in the silence for the sound of breathing. The man had said Lloyd wasn't well. Sam had thought he was lying, but it was possible that Lloyd really wasn't well and had crashed out, or was lying unconscious somewhere. Or he just might not be in the room and Sam was wasting his time, precious time that he didn't have. Maybe he should have run through the house calling Lloyd's name in case he'd been locked in another room, but it was too late for that now.

Please be here, Lloyd, please be here. I don't want to get caught. Please. Where was he? He had to be here. Tears tickled behind Sam's eyes and he swept away the few that made their way down his cheeks.

'Lloyd, Lloyd,' he whispered again, but louder, more urgently. 'It's me. It's Sam. We've got to get out of here. Where are you? Lloyd, stop messing about!'

And then he thought he heard something.

It came from the far corner of the room. He moved towards it, brushing past the bed and over the duvet on the floor. The further he went from the window the less he could see, and he cursed loudly as he stumbled into a small table. A vase fell to the floor with a thump, but somehow Sam managed to catch the table lamp that would have followed it. He could barely see a thing. He put his hands out in front of him and felt the back of a chair. He shuffled round it, and called Lloyd's name again.

He heard a sound, like a whimper or something and it made him stop. It scared him. He stepped back. His heart had started pounding in his ears again. He couldn't do this in the dark. He just couldn't; it was too hard. He struggled with the sudden urge to run away. Why hadn't he just stayed in the woods? Daylight would have come eventually and he could have hidden out until then. Or he could have waited and watched the house until the man left, which he had to do sometime, and then come and got Lloyd.

Sod the risk, he needed light. If he did it carefully, the man might not see it from outside. He backtracked to the small table lamp and found the switch, but he didn't switch it on, not yet. He had to be clever about it. He set the lamp on the floor in front of the chair and felt around for some cushions to place on top of the lamp and around it. There were a couple of cushions on that chair and two on the chair on the other side of the table. Then he switched the lamp on.

Sam had contained the light well. It only lit up the little circle within the cushion ring. He angled the lamp towards the corner where he thought he had heard the sound coming from and then removed the cushion covering the top of the lamp. Now he could use it like a torch.

He peered into the far corners of the room but there was too much stuff in the way to see properly. He crept forwards again and, maybe it was his imagination, but he thought he spotted a slight movement under a side table. Something was under there, and it had to be Lloyd. If it *was* him then why didn't he answer? And what was he doing hiding under a table when he was free to walk out of the house?

The sound of footsteps in the distance penetrated the silence. Sam had almost missed them, but they weren't in his imagination, he was sure of it. The man was coming back and he had to be coming this way. The lamp was still on with its bizarre arrangement of cushions around it, and that would tell the man all he needed to know. He had to switch it off and hide, but Sam couldn't move.

Hide, hide, hide, hide, he screamed at himself, but fear had overcome him and he was paralysed. He couldn't breathe. He couldn't move.

He could hear the man, the ominous tread, the jingle jangle of the keys. Terror gripped hold of Sam and clutched him tight. The dark silent woods were way less frightening than this. He should have stayed out there. He should have burrowed a hole, made himself small, and hidden there. Why had he come back? A scream rose in his throat.

Jingle, jangle, jingle, jangle.

'Sam,' a voice croaked. 'He's coming ...'

And the low timbre of dread-filled moaning started an accompaniment to the jingle jangle.

11

The moaning became a wail as the jingle jangle came closer. The man had reached the outer room. In a few strides he'd be in the bedroom. Sam moved. He scrambled under the bed and pulled the duvet up against the bottom of it. Then he tried not to scream. He clapped his hand over his mouth and screwed his eyes shut tight. But he couldn't keep his eyes shut because then he wouldn't know if the man was looking under the bed. He opened them, and waited.

The main lights came on. Sam could hear laboured breathing as the man lumbered past the bed. He held his own breath until the man had gone past, hoping the man hadn't heard him.

'Been having a wander about, have you?' the man said. 'Told you not to bother, phone's been cut off for months. Seems your friend has taken a walk, too. Can't do as you're told, can you?'

The wailing stopped abruptly.

'Come on, out you come.'

Sam didn't think Lloyd had done as he was told because the man was getting angrier.

'Don't take all day about it, I haven't got much time. Get out of there!'

Sam cringed as the yelling started.

'I told you to come out. Now get the hell out or I'll drag you out myself!'

There was whimpering and shuffling. Sam pulled the duvet down just a tiny bit, just enough to peek out with one eye. He didn't want to see much, but he needed to see a bit. He needed to see Lloyd. Through the tiny peephole, all he could make out was the lower half of the man's body, and then a boy, crawling on his hands and knees, came into view. Sam almost didn't recognise Lloyd. He looked different, and it wasn't just because of the purple bruising round his left eye.

The man slumped down in the chair, his back to Sam, and beckoned with his finger. 'Come closer, Lloyd, we're going to have a little talk and I want you to listen to me carefully. I've got to go out for a bit, but I know you won't do anything silly. Not as stupid as your pal, are you? You know the only way out of here is with me, and like I said, you'll be going home tomorrow – if you're a very, very good boy.'

'I'll be good. I promise I'll be good. I promise. I won't do anything silly. I won't go wandering. I'll stay right here and wait for you. You can trust me. I promise. I promise.' His voice was barely a whisper and Sam had to strain to catch what Lloyd had said.

He knew Lloyd wouldn't let on that Sam was there. He knew he wouldn't dob him in. But Lloyd was scared and if the man threatened him, he just might tell on Sam. The man might promise to take Lloyd home now and Lloyd might be taken in again. If it was the other way around and Sam was out there and Lloyd was under the bed, would the promise of going home make Sam tell? Sam didn't know, but he wanted to think that it would be a no.

No, he'd never tell, and Lloyd wouldn't either. They were wise to that now. Somehow, Sam doubted that anyone would ever be able to take them in again. Ever.

'When I get back you can show me what a good boy you are, eh? We'll have ourselves a bit more fun before you go home. What do you say?'

Lloyd nodded, but his eyes were blank. 'Can I go home afterwards?'

''Course you can,' the man said softly. 'Didn't I promise you that? Didn't I?'

'Yes,' Lloyd whispered.

'As long as you're good, Lloyd. You know I don't want to hurt you, but if you don't listen then I have to help you listen, don't I? I'll get you some ice for your eye when I get back. Doesn't hurt too much, does it?'

'No.'

'Now come over here. Nothing to be scared of. Closer. That's better, Lloyd. Much better. I told you you'd start to like it, didn't I?'

The man began caressing Lloyd, stroking his hair. 'You really are such a good kid,' the man sighed. 'Almost a shame you have to go home, isn't it?'

Sam squeezed his eyes shut and pressed his hands over his ears. He didn't want to hear, he didn't want to see. He felt sick. He began to retch silently, trying hard not to chuck up, trying hard not to make a sound, not to give himself away. Inside he was crying.

He didn't know how long he stayed like that. It could have been just a few minutes, or it could have been an hour. When he took his hands away from his ears he heard the man saying, 'Just to make sure you don't do anything silly and jeopardise your chance of getting home, I'm going to tie your hands. Make yourself comfortable on the bed, Lloyd, that way you can have a kip, too.'

They moved across to the bed and Sam edged his way deeper into the middle of it, desperately hoping the man didn't bend down to pick up the duvet.

'I'll just tie one hand to the bedpost, Lloyd, so you're not uncomfortable. There now, that didn't hurt, did it?'

He sounded so nice, so attentive, so considerate. He could have been a doctor, and not a complete whacko psycho sicko maniac.

Lloyd's response was a muffled no.

'Good. Right, I'll be back in a bit.'

The man started moving away from the bed. Sam held

his breath, willing him to walk out of the room without stopping. But he did stop because the duvet was swept up off the floor. Sam made himself as small as possible, and felt the weight of the marble in his hand. He didn't remember taking it out of his pocket, but he must have at some point. He almost wished the man would bend down and stick his head under the bed. Sam would have got a perfect hit. He clenched his teeth, anger and a hatred he had never experienced before welled up from deep inside him, and he saw the scene in his head. Smash! Smash! Smash! Blood spilling out everywhere. Smash! Life oozing out of the man, draining away. Death. And then Lloyd and him would be free.

But the man didn't bend down to check under the bed because he thought that Sam had escaped and he was on his way to hunt him down.

'There, now you won't get cold,' the man said. 'I'll bring us back some pizza, or burgers, if you like. Have to keep your strength up,' he chuckled. And then he was gone.

Sam didn't move for a while. He listened carefully to the footsteps receding into the distance until he couldn't hear them any more. Then came the faint sound of a door slamming, and then after another minute the squeal of tyres outside. Time to move.

He crawled out from under the bed, blinking as the blazing light hit his eyes. He had spent too much time in darkness. He went towards Lloyd. His friend was lying on his side, his knees drawn up to his chest, his back to Sam, but one arm raised back at an awkward angle, tied to the bedpost. Sam put a hand on Lloyd's shoulder and felt his friend cringe away from his touch. He felt Lloyd's fear, the trembling and uncontrollable shaking, and it was like Lloyd was lying in an Arctic plain instead of under a warm duvet, in a warm bed, in a warm room.

Fear made you cold. It made you tremble. Anger made you hot. It made you want to hurt someone.

Sam fumbled with the knot that held Lloyd to the bed. He had thought the man was a bit stupid tying only one hand – Lloyd could have untied it with his other hand. But the knot didn't have a simple bow that you could just pull and hey presto you were free; it was tight, triple knotted with no bow. The man wouldn't have been unable to untie it. Maybe he never meant to untie it.

Sam struggled with it, but he knew he'd never be able to undo the knots. The bedpost was a fussy ornate thing topped with a round ball. If Sam could knock the stupid ball off, he might be able to slide the rope up and off the post. He tested it. It appeared to be carved from the same piece of wood as the rest of the bed frame and not glued on afterwards. No way he'd be able to knock it off without a hammer, and he didn't have a hammer. He cast about the room for something heavy that he could use instead. At the far end of the room were a collection of vases and little statues displayed in a glass cabinet. They looked expensive; they looked like they might be heavy enough.

Sam left Lloyd's side and crossed quickly to the cabinet. It wasn't locked. He opened the doors and started picking out the pieces that looked heavy. He weighed them in his hands and realised that none of them were that heavy, but he had to give them a go because there was nothing else in the room that looked remotely useful. Nothing. Not a single stupid thing. How was he going to get Lloyd free? How were they going to get away before the man gave up looking for Sam and came back for Lloyd?

Sam plucked all the smaller vases out of the cabinet and let them fall to the floor, the bigger ones he took in both hands and smashed down on top of the pile until every single vase lay in tiny shards and splinters on the floor. He gazed at his handiwork, and hoped the stuff had been worth a fortune. He went back to the bed with the heavier objects; one of them, he hoped, would knock the bedpost off the bed. He dropped the collection onto the bed. Lloyd hadn't moved. He hadn't even turned his head when Sam had started smashing things.

'Okay, Lloyd, I'm going to try and bash the top of the bedpost off, so there's going to a bit of a racket.'

He selected the heavy wooden lion carving first. The lion had its head tossed back and its mouth was wide open in mid-roar. Sam gripped its back legs and swung with all his might. The lion's head flew off and smacked the wall with a thud. There was a slight indentation in the bedpost, nothing more. He swung again, and again, making more marks in the wood, but the bed knob hadn't shifted. He tried the other pieces, but knew it was a dead loss. This idea wasn't going to work.

He needed something to cut through the rope with. He needed a sharp knife, and somehow he knew he wasn't going to find one in this room. He didn't have a choice. He had to leave Lloyd and find the kitchen.

'Lloyd, I can't knock the bed knob off and I can't undo the stupid knot.'

Lloyd didn't respond.

'I'm going to go and find a knife. Okay? I'll be back as soon as I can. Lloyd?'

Still Lloyd didn't answer. He hadn't said a word since the man had gone.

'Lloyd, I'm coming back.'

Sam turned and left the room, only one thing on his mind now. A knife. He didn't look back.

12

Back out of the bedroom and into the TV room, where he stopped for a moment. The camcorder was still sitting on its tripod, facing the overstuffed sofa with its plump, overstuffed cushions. He knew how camcorders worked. It didn't take him more than a second to remove the little tape from inside it and stuff it deep into the pocket of his school trousers. He shuddered. It made him feel cold. It made him feel scared.

Knife. He had to find a knife. He was on the move again.

Back down the corridor, swiftly past the doors that stood wide open to the yawning darkness within them. It wouldn't be any good searching through them now. There was no phone. No one at the end of the line. Knife. He needed to find a knife. At the first set of stairs he stopped. The kitchen would be downstairs at the back somewhere. He might be lucky and find it at the bottom of this flight of stairs. They led into a forbidding darkness, but Sam didn't mind that so much now. He headed down.

At the bottom, he groped around for a light switch and flicked it on. He was standing in a corridor, but it wasn't lined with any pictures, or paintings, or anything. It just had plain, unadorned walls. That meant he was close. People who lived in houses like this didn't cook for themselves. They probably didn't even know where the kitchen was. They had cooks and butlers and servants, and you didn't waste nice stuff on them. The first door he got to was a big cupboard full of brooms and mops and polish and rags. The second door was a storeroom with shelves upon shelves of plates and cups and bowls and linens. The third door was the kitchen.

Sam switched on the light and let his eyes travel across the work surfaces. The man had left a mess. Open packets of food and wrappers were strewn on one of the surfaces, and on another were bags of chips and chicken nuggets, and a half-eaten pizza. He spotted the knife block next to the hob. It contained ten knives in an assortment of sizes. Sam found a tea towel and took every single knife. He wrapped them up carefully and hid the empty block in a cupboard. Then he retraced his steps back to Lloyd. This time he didn't leave any doors open, or lights switched on.

He didn't know how much time he had left. He should have checked his watch when the man had driven off, but he hadn't, which was stupid of him and he could have kicked himself for it. Everything hinged on getting Lloyd free and getting out of the house before the man returned. The man would have shut the main gate after he went out, and driven down the long, windy track back to the road. Sooner or later he would realise that a kid couldn't climb the gate and jump off the other side – it would have been a tough task for a grown-up to have done. He'd know he'd been tricked, and then he would come speeding back.

Sam's watch now said four o'clock. Daylight was only a few hours away. They had to get out quick, and find somewhere to hide until dawn. Somewhere safe. But first he had to free Lloyd.

'It's me, Lloyd,' Sam said as he entered the bedroom. 'I've got some knives.'

Lloyd didn't look up.

Sam set the tea towel on the bed and unfolded it to reveal his treasure. He picked a heavy, serrated knife from the collection and started sawing through the knot. It was hard work even though the knife was sharp. Sam sawed faster, backwards and forwards, backwards and forwards. It was starting to go through the rope. More effort, more speed, that's what it needed. And then Lloyd would be free.

He took a firm grip of the rope, pulling the end that was attached to Lloyd's hand as taut as he could, and then he went faster, his hand a blur of motion, and at first he didn't feel the place where the knife had sliced through his hand and almost taken his thumb off. Blood dripped down and onto the bed, tons of it. He stared down at the sheet paralysed as it gradually went from white to red as his hot pulsing blood continued to flood out of the gaping smile he'd sliced into his hand. And then he felt the pain.

Searing pain, blinding pain, followed an intense agonised cry. Sam had never felt pain like that before. The knife fell from his right hand. He clutched at his left wrist, his body doubled over as spasms of pain shuddered through him. His knees buckled beneath him and he sank down to the floor. He couldn't work out whether he was going to faint or be sick, or both.

He closed his eyes and leaned his head against the side of the bed. He sobbed until the spasms no longer racked right through him. He opened his eyes and pressed his bloodied hand against the bed, teeth gritted against the pain from the pressure. Then he forced himself to look closely at his wound. His thumb wasn't hanging off by a thread of skin as he had feared. It was still firmly attached to his hand. The wound was ugly but not deep, and Sam was suddenly so angry with himself. How could he have let that happen? How could he have been so stupid? He'd just begun to make progress. He'd been so close to getting Lloyd freed from the bed. It wasn't fair. It just wasn't fair. How had he ended up in this mess? Why him? Why them? Why? Tears ran down his face and he swiped at them not caring that he was smearing blood across his face.

But he wasn't going to let the man win. And he wasn't going to leave the house without Lloyd.

He shook the tea towel free of the knives, letting them fall to the floor, and wrapped the towel tightly around his hand. He picked up the serrated knife with its bloodied blade and began sawing again, sobbing with every stroke of the blade, his left hand clutched against his chest. But it wasn't working like that. He had to use his left hand to hold the other end of the rope. He almost cried out with pain when he gripped hold of the rope and pulled it taut. He started again. And then suddenly he was through. The rope was cut in two and Lloyd's arm slumped to the bed. He'd done it! Lloyd was free.

'Lloyd, get up. We've got to go. We've got to get out of here.'

The same silence greeted Sam. He shook Lloyd's shoulder hard. There was no response. He pulled him round to face him. Blank, empty eyes. Lloyd had gone somewhere deep inside himself. Sam was afraid he wasn't going to come back any time soon.

'Lloyd, please get up. He could be back any minute. We've got to get out.'

Lloyd blinked. It wasn't much, but it was a sign. That's all Sam needed. He began to pull the duvet and the sheets back, but somehow Lloyd moved faster and held on to them tight. Sam stared at him.

'What are you doing, you idiot? We've got to leave. Don't you understand? He's not going to take you home, stupid. He's going to kill you!' Sam shouted into Lloyd's face. 'He's already tried to kill me! So don't be a—'

Lloyd's mouth moved, but Sam couldn't hear what Lloyd had tried to say because Sam couldn't stop shouting.

'We don't have time for this crap. Just get up. Get up!' he screamed, and yanked the covers back. Then he saw why Lloyd wouldn't get up.

Lloyd drew his knees close to his chest, and Sam looked away. He looked round the room and spotted Lloyd's trousers. He brought them back to his friend and placed them on the bed beside him. Then he turned his back.

'Can't find your p—. You know, your other stuff, but it doesn't matter. We're going home, Lloyd. Just as soon as we get out of here.'

Sam heard Lloyd shuffling across the bed and the bedsprings springing back as Lloyd stood up. Sam turned back towards his friend, and said, 'Shit, shoes!' when he saw Lloyd's socked feet. He hunted around the floor and found them tucked under a chair. He helped Lloyd into them and then saw the precious collection of knives on the floor. He pulled his rucksack out from under the bed and chucked them into it. Everything was so much harder with only one hand. His left hand was still wrapped inside the bloody tea towel, which was soaked through. Sam looked round for something else, but couldn't see anything apart from the pillowcases. He tried to get one off, but he couldn't do it without two hands.

'Damn!' he cursed. Sam glanced at Lloyd and knew he couldn't ask him to help.

He gave up the struggle with the pillowcase, and muttered, 'Right, let's go.'

Lloyd didn't say anything but he shambled out after Sam. In the sitting room, Sam spotted Lloyd's coat sticking out of his rucksack and snagged it on the way out. Sam couldn't carry two rucksacks, but Lloyd might need the coat later.

'We have to go a bit faster, Lloyd,' Sam said, stepping up the pace.

The need to get out of the house was overwhelming. The only way out of the house was through the front door. Every other door was bound to be locked, and there was no time to go round checking them now. The front door definitely wouldn't be locked because the man wasn't expecting anyone to go out of it. Sam grabbed Lloyd's sleeve and dragged him along faster. They went flying down the stairs and through the dark corridors. Sam didn't need much light now; he knew his way around this house. Lloyd tripped and stumbled behind him, but kept going as long as Sam led.

They got to the front door. It was shut, which was no surprise as Sam had heard the man slam it on his way out. He opened it a crack and it groaned noisily. Sam winced but opened it some more. The car wasn't back yet. The man was still out hunting.

He took hold of Lloyd's arm again and led him out, remembering to close the door behind them. Then he stopped. His breath formed little clouds of smoke. It had got much colder since he'd been out last. He helped Lloyd into his coat, and then put his own on. He hesitated before hoisting his rucksack onto his back again. It was extra weight. But he decided he didn't want to leave it in the house.

The outside lights were still on, casting long shadows on the lawn, which stretched out towards the trees. He hadn't thought about this bit. He didn't have a plan. He had been so intent on getting Lloyd out of the house that he hadn't thought about what to do next. Where should he take them? Where was it safe? Nowhere was safe, but some places were safer than others.

The woods were good only as long as it was dark. Come daylight the man would scour them easily. They'd have to keep moving, be ahead of him all the time, and in the end he'd see them. The gate. That was the answer. When the man came back and opened the gates, they'd wait until he was through and then dive out of them quickly. He'd only see them if he was looking in his rear-view mirror or his side mirror, and what was the chance of that? But what if he did see them? Then they'd be lost. It wouldn't take the man more than a few seconds to turn his car round and head out after them. From what Sam could remember the hedgerows grew really close on either side of the track, which meant they might not be able to find a way through them. There was no way they could outrun a car, not with Lloyd barely able to walk without help, and not with Sam's dodgy ankle. They would be trapped. But they might find a gap in the hedge and be able to squeeze through it and hide. He'd never find them then. But if they didn't find a gap, he would run them over.

Sam looked at the driveway leading down to the gate, stuck in indecision. Then a thought struck him. Where were the garages and sheds and stuff like that? They weren't part of the house so they had to be somewhere in the grounds. The only section that Sam hadn't been through was the bit between the back of the house, from his bathroom window, going left towards the gate. They had to be down there somewhere. He'd take Lloyd there and they could hide out in a garage or a shed and the man would never find them. He wouldn't think of it. He'd search the house from top to bottom before he'd think of going down to the sheds.

Sam stepped out onto the gravel. 'Come on, Lloyd. We're going to find a safe place to hide.'

13

Sam followed the gravel driveway around the side of the house to the back. A bit further on there was a large building, and as they got closer to it, Sam saw that it was a set of linked garages, their shiny silver doors luminous like sheets of ice. Above the garages was a bank of dark windows. Servants' quarters maybe, or the driver's rooms. Sam quickly decided that they couldn't hide there. For a start, it was still way too close to the house, and once they were inside the rooms, they might not be able to get out. They would be trapped. On the other hand, the man might not even think of looking for them there.

Now Sam couldn't decide. Everything had its pros and cons, but this was not just any decision, this was the most important decision of Sam's life. He had to get it right, didn't he? Their lives depended on it.

The soft purr of a car engine reached Sam's ears as the rain came down. The man was back already. Behind him, Lloyd had begun to whimper. Sam didn't know what to do next, but he knew one thing – if they didn't move away from the garages fast, they might get spotted, especially if the man decided to park the car round the back. He pulled Lloyd along, towards the garages at first, until he saw the path. It ran alongside the building and Sam followed it round to the back and stayed on it as it led them away from the building towards the trees. They were a good distance away from the house now and the darkness was much thicker, but Sam was glad of it. The darkness made him feel a bit safer. He just wished he had a torch. He should have looked for one in the kitchen. Everyone kept a torch in the kitchen. Too late to go back for one now.

He kept to the path, following it into the trees where it narrowed and became a grassy track. The trees sheltered them from the steady drizzle, Sam couldn't hear the car engine any more, and Lloyd had stopped whimpering. The only sound was their breathing and the rustling of leaves as the rain pitter-pattered on them. Sam kept hold of Lloyd's sleeve – he had to because when he let go Lloyd stopped and didn't move. He just stood there and waited for Sam to come back for him.

They came to a clearing where the light of the moon shone through brightly and they could see that someone had used this area to cut logs. There were wheelbarrows, a very large lawnmower, the kind you sit on and drive, and a bunch of sheds huddled around the far side of the clearing.

It was what Sam had been looking for, but now he wasn't so sure about the idea. They would be trapped again, wouldn't they, and in an even smaller, confined space. It had been a stupid plan. Why hadn't he thought that bit through? He slumped down on the stump of a tree. Lloyd stayed standing, stayed silent, waiting. Sam put his head in his hands as he finally realised that nowhere would have been a good enough hiding place. He wouldn't have felt safe anywhere. They would never be safe as long as they were within the wrought-iron, barbed-wire-topped, too-high fence, which couldn't be climbed and couldn't be squeezed through.

He couldn't just sit there and do nothing. Sam looked at the sheds again. Maybe it wasn't such a bad idea to hide in one of them. At least they would be out of the rain. He pushed off the tree stump and went to have a closer look at them. There were five sheds, two of them double the size of the others, and all of them unlocked. The larger ones were stacked with garden furniture, chairs, tables, umbrellas, recliners, and an assortment of garden games and paddling pools, and gardening tools lined neatly against the wall. Sam didn't bother checking the smaller sheds; no way was he going to hide in one of those. He picked one of the two bigger ones and went back for Lloyd.

Lloyd was standing with his hands hanging beside him, his eyes looking straight ahead, but not at anything in particular. Sam wished Lloyd would look at him, say something, even a nod or shake of his head would have done for starters. He knew Lloyd could hear him though, so he didn't stop talking to him, response or no response.

Once Sam got Lloyd far, far away from this hell hole he would be fine, back to his old self again.

'Come on, Lloyd. I've found somewhere for us to hide out,' Sam whispered.

He took Lloyd's hand and led him across to the shed and through the door. He closed the door behind them. It was still and quiet inside, and dark. The shed had two large windows facing into the clearing that allowed the moonlight in, but Sam couldn't make anything out. He had to open the door again while he found a good place to hide inside. He wanted a secret cupboard, a little nook, a concealed space where the man would never find them.

Sam found one at the back of the shed. Behind stacks of chairs and folded tables there was a little cubbyhole just big enough for two kids. It was perfect. There was no way the man would see them unless he was right up close. On his way back to close the door, Sam spotted a cupboard, which he discovered contained stacks of green garden chair cushions. Amazingly they weren't too damp and mouldy. He grabbed a handful and tossed them onto the floor of their cubbyhole, and that's when he noticed the other door.

A back way out. An escape route, Sam thought, glad he'd picked this shed now. But no, not really much of an escape route because if they had to use it then it meant the man had almost caught them anyway. It also meant that Sam would have to watch two entrances.

He got Lloyd to sit down on the cushions, and quickly glanced round for anything else that might be useful, but nothing else jumped out at him. He hurried back and closed the shed door, wishing there was a lock, or a bolt or something. But there wasn't, which was probably just as well because a shed bolted from the inside would have been a real giveaway. Sam thought he must be tired. All his thoughts were beginning to get jumbled up and nothing was making sense any more; he wasn't making sense. He made his way back to the cubbyhole and pulled the stack of chairs closer in once he was inside. Snug.

They sat quietly, shoulder to shoulder, listening to the sound of nothing. *Nothing* can sound very loud sometimes, louder than noise, even louder than a jumbo jet passing overhead.

'You okay, Lloyd?' Sam asked eventually.

Lloyd lifted his shoulders a fraction, but maintained his silence. His eyes were dark pools, unreadable, expressionless, or just wide open because maybe Lloyd was afraid of closing them.

'We're safe here, Lloyd, and we're together, so, you know, it's okay. Everything's going to be okay.' That sounded lame, but Sam didn't know what else to say. 'We'll be fine now as long as we stick together.'

He knew Lloyd was suffering from extreme shock, or something, but he didn't really know what to do, apart from try and keep them safe, and then try and escape, and then try and get them home. There was too much to do. Home felt like it was in a different land, in a different country, and Sam didn't know the way.

Sam's eyes began to close and he struggled to keep them open. Next to him, Lloyd's eyes had finally closed. Sam knew he had to keep watch just in case the man finished searching the house and decided to search the grounds next, but staying awake was becoming increasingly difficult. Even the persistent ache from his throbbing thumb wasn't helping to keep his eyes open for more than a minute at a time. The pain extended from his index finger, across the base of his thumb and down the side of his hand. The pain told him it was a nasty cut. But in the darkness, Sam couldn't see how deep it was, or how bloody his hands were. Sam wondered whether the wound would get infected and he would end up dying in the cubbyhole, his body discovered only years later by new tenants, with Lloyd still sitting beside him.

He fell asleep.

When he woke up the shed was full of light. The sun had come up and dried up all the rain. Lloyd was still sleeping. Sam listened to the silence, listened hard for any sound or noise from outside the shed. He couldn't hear anything. A glance at his watch told him that it was only eight o'clock. Then he noticed his hands, both smeared with dried blood, and the cut, deeper and uglier than he thought it would be. And then the terrible, agonising pain registered in his brain. The wound must have reopened while he was asleep because there was blood on his trousers and on the cushions. The tea towel had fallen off.

Sam hunted around for it, but there was no sign of it, unless it was under Lloyd and Sam didn't think it was there. He'd dropped it. Somewhere. Idiot! What if he'd bled all the way down from the house to the sheds and had left a trail for the man to follow. Little drops of blood, a trail of crumbling children – would *he* see them in the light of day? Maybe not, but a blood-soaked tea towel would be conspicuous. A red rag – how could the man resist it? If Sam had dropped it on the way down, the man would know where to find them.

No, he can't have dropped it outside; it had to be in the shed. Sam crawled out from the cubbyhole, careful not to wake Lloyd up. Lloyd with the black-blue-purple eye, which had swollen up grotesquely overnight. As Sam left the cubbyhole, a hand grabbed his ankle.

'Don't leave me.'

'I'm not,' Sam snapped as his heart leapt into his mouth. Lloyd had scared him for a minute. He'd thought he was asleep. 'Sorry. I'm not leaving you, Lloyd. I'm just looking for the stupid towel I used to wrap my hand up in. I've dropped it, and I don't know where,' Sam explained.

Lloyd shook his head, his eyes pleading.

'I've got to find it, Lloyd, because if I dropped it outside the shed, he'll find us.'

'It could be anywhere.'

Lloyd was right, Sam thought. It could be anywhere. But if it was inside the shed, then their hiding place was still safe. If it wasn't then they had to get out of there.

'I know, but I've got to take a look. I'm not leaving the shed. Honest.'

Sam crawled out and this time Lloyd didn't try to stop him. He went through the whole shed, from front to back, looking under everything, looking on top of everything, even checking inside the cupboard in case it had somehow got lodged between the seat pads, but he didn't find it. He kind of knew he wouldn't. Luck came and went, randomly. It was gone at the moment, or maybe it was there, and that was what was keeping them alive. No, Sam didn't think it was that. He'd kept himself alive, with a little help from luck; and with a bit more help from luck, he was going to make sure he and Lloyd stayed that way.

Lloyd was already doing better now that he was away from the house. He had started talking again; he'd only said a couple of sentences so far, but that was a good sign. As long as the man didn't come anywhere near them, Lloyd would be fine. And he wouldn't – not unless that stupid tea towel was sitting on the ground outside their shed pointing the way out to him.

Sam crept up to one of the windows and looked out. The glass was smudged and grimy with a host of cobwebs, but that was just fine because Sam liked spiders, the bigger the better, but it also meant that no one could see into the shed easily, and Sam could see the whole of the clearing and would know if anyone was out there.

There was no one there. He watched and waited for a long while, just to be sure there was no one waiting to jump out from behind a tree and grab him. Sam wasn't going to be lulled into a false sense of security because he'd forgotten what the word *security* meant. *Wariness* he knew very well.

Right, Sam, stop procrastinating, it's all clear out there and you've got no excuse. Get it over with.

Because what Sam couldn't see properly was the ground outside the shed, and he knew what he had to do.

14

'Lloyd, I've got to go out for a second,' Sam whispered. 'Just for a second. I promise. I'll be back in a minute. You'll be fine.'

Lloyd didn't reply. He was curled up in a tight ball, shivering, silent. He needed a hot bath and a warm, cosy bed to snuggle up inside, but all Sam could give him was a hard, damp floor and some empty words of hope. It wasn't much.

'Don't make a sound – no matter what you hear. And ... and just in case anything does happen, there's a back door over there. Use it if you have to, and then run like mad,' Sam added. He suddenly realised he didn't sound like an eleven-year-old any more. He sounded more like a dad, or something, which felt crazy. Mad.

He didn't think Lloyd had heard anything he'd said, but he hoped he had. If the man was somewhere outside, Sam's great plan, which wasn't really a great plan but the only thing he could think of, was to lead him away from Lloyd. There was no sense in them both getting caught, and Lloyd could get away and hide in the woods until someone came looking for them. They had to be looking for them, didn't they? They'd been missing for a whole night. The entire police force would be out searching for them, asking everyone questions about them. Someone had to have seen the big, shiny, flash set of wheels whisking them away, and how many big, shiny, flash sets of wheels could there be in this area? There couldn't be many.

Sam opened the door a crack, but not wide enough to be able to see much of the ground. He had to open it wider, but very, very slowly, inch by inch with no sudden movements that might attract the eye, *his* eye. He waited a minute and then opened it another few inches, and after another long pause, another couple of inches. It was a bright autumn day outside, the leaves glowing rich russets and oranges and golden hues, the sky a bright, cloudless blue, the air crisp. Perfect day for a walk. But there was nothing perfect about the walk Sam was going to have to take. For a start it wasn't going to be a walk, it was going to be a sprint, and it was probably the stupidest thing he could have done, but it made sense to him.

Okay, now he could see the whole clearing. He scanned it for the bloody towel. It should have been easy to spot. Bright red and drenched with blood. Sam saw it, but it wasn't bright red any more, more of a reddish brown colour. It was over by the tree stump in the middle of the clearing. He knew he had to get it. He knew it was the only thing that would tell the man where they were hiding. He had to get it. The thing was, it was just so far away.

He hesitated; no, it wasn't hesitation, he was being cautious; no, he was being clever, that's what it was. And maybe a bit afraid. Maybe a lot afraid. Count it out, Sam, he told himself, it was the only way he could make himself leave the safety of the shed. On the count of three he was going to belt across the clearing, pick up the towel, and belt back, and he was going to try and do it in less than five seconds. That was a heck of a challenge, but Sam quite liked racing: well, he used to.

He took a deep breath, his eyes on the path that led from the garages down through the trees and into the clearing, willing it to stay empty for the next several seconds. Then he counted to three. Then he ran. One Mississippi, two Mississippi, three Mississippi, he was halfway across the clearing; four Mississippi, five Mississippi – he hadn't made his target, but he'd got the rag and he was on his way back. Seven Mississippi, eight Mississippi, nine and he was back at the door, out of breath and the blood screaming in his ears.

He checked the clearing and the trees for any movement before stepping back inside the shed, resisting the temptation to slam the door shut and block it up with everything he could lay his hands on. He closed the door very slowly, keeping watch until the crack was too small to see through. Then he went to the window and kept a lookout from there.

No one was going to creep up on them without Sam knowing about it.

The next time he looked at his watch it said twelve thirty, which didn't feel right. Had he been keeping watch at the window for that long? He must have been. His fingers were completely numb and he couldn't feel his feet at all. In his left hand a dull throb had replaced the excruciating pain he'd woken up with, so at least the cold had been good for something. There had been no movement from outside at all, which meant the man was searching other areas of the grounds, or maybe he was still searching the house. Sam looked out one more time and then tore himself away from the window and went to check on Lloyd.

Lloyd was as Sam had left him: curled up with his arms hugging his knees and his head resting on top of them.

'I got the towel. It was in the clearing outside, but it's okay. No one saw me.'

Lloyd blinked in response.

'I think we'll be safe here for a bit,' Sam continued.

Suddenly he felt completely drained. He needed to sit down. He crawled under the tables and chairs and nestled up close to Lloyd. They shivered together.

'The police will be looking for us. It won't be long before they find us. Maybe we should stay here until they do. What do you think, Lloyd?'

Lloyd shrugged. It wasn't much of a response, but then there wasn't much of a choice: hide out there, or hide out somewhere else. That was it.

'I don't know either,' Sam sighed. He was too tired to think. He closed his eyes. He needed to rest them for a few minutes.

He must have drifted off into a deep, dreamless sleep because the little nudge woke him with a start. The shed was darker. It must have got cloudier outside or maybe it was late and he'd slept all day. Sam glanced at Lloyd. He had his finger pressed against his lips, and only then did Sam become aware of the shuffling outside. Someone was out there. Someone was looking for them, and he didn't think it was the police. There would have been lots of them, all calling their names loudly. This sounded like one person. Sam felt trapped now. They should have gone into the woods and found a tree, or a hollow to hide in, or dug a hole and buried themselves inside it.

They both held their breath, and neither of them moved, not even to blink their eyes. The sound of footsteps went round the shed, passing behind them, and then they disappeared. Still, neither boy moved, or spoke, or breathed. The footsteps returned, and then the shed door opened. Lloyd reached for Sam's hand and clutched it hard. Sam could feel Lloyd's fear mingling with his own.

Please don't make a sound, Lloyd. Please don't make a sound, Sam cried fervently inside his head. If they kept quiet, the man wouldn't hear them and he would go away and search somewhere else. He didn't know they were hiding there. Or had he guessed?

They heard his heavy tread on the wooden boards of the shed. The boards creaked and made snapping noises underfoot; he was coming further into the shed. There was scraping and bumping noises as he shifted bits of furniture, looking, searching.

'Come out, come out, wherever you are,' he sang.

Sam felt the spasm of fear and loathing that shot through Lloyd. He clutched his hand harder and looked directly into Lloyd's eyes, telling him to make no sound, telling him to make no movement. But Lloyd's lips were quivering uncontrollably.

'Come out, Lloyd. Time to go home,' the man said. 'Come on out, Lloyd.'

Lloyd closed his eyes, but his body leaned forward as though he was about to get up and crawl out of the cubbyhole. Sam panicked and held onto his friend hard. He had to stop him because Lloyd wasn't thinking straight. When the man was around, he just did whatever the man told him to do.

Sam was sure the man didn't know they were there, but he wished he would stop singing that stupid song. He was just trying his luck; trying to entice Lloyd out with promises of going home. Did he really think they were stupid enough to believe his lies? The man hadn't bothered calling for him though, Sam thought. Maybe he thought Sam had got away, or maybe he knew that Sam wasn't afraid of him in the same way Lloyd was. He had no power over Sam, not like he had over Lloyd.

The footsteps went backwards and forwards a few more times, but after a few minutes, they clomped back towards the door, and didn't come back again. Sam kept hold of Lloyd for a long time, even when Lloyd's body went limp as the fear seeped away. The man had gone, but he had left the shed door wide open. Sam let go of Lloyd and saw that his watch said quarter to five. He *had* slept all day. And no one, other than the man, had come looking for them. They'd been missing a whole night and a whole day now. How much longer would they have to wait before they were rescued? Would they even *be* rescued?

They had had a close call, and Sam had no idea whether the man would come back to the shed again. What should they do? Should he take Lloyd into the woods and hide out there. But it was a freezing cold night. What to do, where to go? Sam let his head fall into his hands and he cried. He hadn't cried since the night before, but now all he wanted to do was cry and cry and cry. He did it quietly, without making a sound. He didn't want the man to hear; he didn't want him to come back to the shed. After a while the tears stopped. Lloyd hadn't said a word.

Sam wiped his nose on his sleeve, and said, 'You hungry, Lloyd?'

Lloyd shrugged, and Sam took that to mean yes. He had stuffed a muffin and a banana in his coat pocket at lunch at school. Yesterday. It had only been yesterday, but it had been the longest weekend of Sam's life – and it was only Saturday evening. The banana and the muffin would have to keep them going, as he hadn't thought of swiping any food from the kitchen in the house. All he'd thought about then was finding a sharp knife. He dug into his pocket and found the battered muffin and bruised banana, but they were edible and that's what mattered. He divided them out between them.

'Just have to imagine they're something else,' Sam suggested.

They ate slowly. Both of them knew there wasn't anything else to eat after this.

'It'll keep us going until tomorrow,' Sam said. 'The police will find us by then.'

'No, they won't,' Lloyd said in a matter-of-fact tone.

Sam turned to face Lloyd. 'Yes, they will, Lloyd.'

'You don't have to pretend any more, Sam.'

'I'm not pretending,' Sam insisted. 'They're looking for us, and they're going to find us. It's just a matter of surviving until they do.'

'We're going to die here.'

'Don't be stupid! "Course we're not!' Sam hissed angrily. 'We're getting out of here alive!'

'If you say so, Sam,' Lloyd replied, his voice had dropped to a whisper. He sounded defeated.

'I do. I do,' Sam repeated.

They sat without speaking for a while. Outside it got darker and then night fell. The shed door still stood wide open and there was nothing Sam could do about it. He desperately wanted to get up and shut it, but he knew he couldn't do that. They moved closer together as the air turned chilly. It was going to be a clear night, which meant frost, which meant it was going to get colder and colder. Would they freeze to death? Sam wondered. Maybe that was what the man was hoping: that they were in the woods and would freeze to death, and he'd come out in the morning and find their frozen bodies. He wouldn't have to bother killing them then.

They weren't going to die. Help was coming, but what if it came too late for them?

Sam needed another plan.

15

A good plan. Easier said than done, Sam thought. What were their options? To stay in the shed, or to leave the shed. They couldn't stay in the shed forever. Why not? asked the other voice in Sam's head. The man might come back and tear the place apart and then he'd find them, or he might torch all the sheds, or there might be guard dogs in a kennel somewhere in the grounds and he might set them loose on them. The man was capable of anything. He was a monster. Sam thought he might be hallucinating now, but were they such far-fetched theories? Sam didn't think they were, although now he thought about it maybe there weren't any dogs because if there were, he would have heard them barking.

Sam needed the loo, even though he hadn't drunk anything since the night before. Lloyd probably needed the loo, too. Well, they could always find a corner of the shed to piss in, so they didn't have to leave their hideout for that. Sam rubbed his temples with his good hand. His head had started hurting and it made it really hard to think properly.

He just wanted to stay where he was. He didn't want to go out into the cold, dark night – not with the man somewhere out there searching for them.

He'd ask Lloyd. 'We need a plan, Lloyd,' he said.

Lloyd shifted his position next to him, but didn't say anything. Sam had expected that.

'We need to get out of here. Out of the grounds. We need to find the road, or some houses, or something. No one knows we're here.'

'*He* knows.'

'Yeah, but he doesn't know we're hiding in here,' Sam replied.

'He'll find us.'

'No. He won't. He's already looked here once. He won't come back.'

'How do you know?'

'I just do.'

'He won't give up.'

'I know. That's why we need to get out of here,' Sam said. 'We need an escape plan.'

Lloyd lapsed into silence again, which Sam took to mean he couldn't think of anything either.

'I've already gone round the fence most of the way round the edge of the grounds, and there was no way through it. It's too high for us to climb, but we could dig under it, maybe. What do you think? Lloyd?'

After a long pause when Sam thought Lloyd wasn't going to answer, Lloyd said, 'Okay.'

'Okay,' Sam repeated. If Lloyd hadn't said okay, Sam would have happily stayed in the shed. But Lloyd had said okay, so now Sam had to sort out the rest of the plan. Digging stuff, implements, weren't going to be a problem as Sam knew where they were kept. Getting them wasn't going to be too special though as Sam would have to go alone. He didn't *have* to go alone, but it was the sensible thing to do. He couldn't drag Lloyd round on a tour of the sheds.

'I think there are shovels and stuff in the other big shed. I'll go and get a couple and meet you round the back of this shed. Count to a hundred, that'll give me enough time to get the stuff, and when you get to a hundred come out. Use the back door, and just wait for me. We'll head into the woods together. If you hear him, go back and hide in the cubbyhole, or if it's too late for that, then head for the woods without me. Have you got that?'

'Yes,' Lloyd said. 'But ...'

'But what?'

'Can't we do it in the morning? When it's light?'

'He'd see us, wouldn't he? He can't see us in the dark.'

'But we can't see him either.'

'We'll take it in turns to dig while the other one keeps a lookout from a hiding place in the trees,' Sam suggested. 'That way he won't be able to sneak up on us. And besides we'll be armed with a shovel. He won't know what's hit him. Okay? Lloyd?'

Lloyd nodded.

Sam crawled out of the cubbyhole first and Lloyd followed. He directed Lloyd towards the far corner where the back door was and headed towards the front to the open door himself. Outside it was pitch black. Sam couldn't see anything. He suddenly didn't want to go out through the open door, but he knew he had to. Lloyd was already counting to a hundred. Sam stepped out of the shed, his back hugging the wall. He half-expected a torch to be switched on in his face and someone to say, 'Gotcha!', and just the thought of that paralysed him for a minute. Fear did that to you, even just the thought of it. It stopped you from functioning. But Sam couldn't let it stop him now.

He moved quickly towards the other shed and threw himself across the open space between the two sheds. He squatted down and crawled through the wide-open door. Propped up against the wall was a collection of gardening implements. Sam groped through them, looking for two shovels. He found one and laid it down on the floor beside him. Lloyd must have got to about sixty now in the count and Sam still couldn't find another shovel. He found a small trowel and a potting fork and laid them down next to the shovel, counting in his head from sixty. When he got to ninety, he gave up looking and picked up what he had. It was time to get going.

He crawled out of the open door and went round the side of the shed before standing up. Then he ran, hunched over, to where Lloyd was waiting behind the other shed, except when Sam got there, Lloyd wasn't there. He dropped the stuff on the ground next to the wall and tried the door. It was locked or bolted from the inside.

'Lloyd? Lloyd?' Sam whispered through the door.

There was no response.

Sam thought he heard a twig snapping underfoot somewhere behind him and swung round. There was no one there. He bent down and picked up the potting fork. Now he was armed. He kept it in his right hand while he made his way round to the front of the shed and back through the open door.

'Lloyd? Lloyd? It's me, Sam.'

'Sam, it's locked,' Lloyd whispered back from the darkness.

Sam had assumed it wouldn't be locked. Why would you lock one of the shed doors and leave the other one unlocked? It didn't make sense. Sam didn't have time to make any sense out of it.

'I'll take you out the front. Hurry up,' Sam whispered back.

Sam kept watch while Lloyd made his way through the shed. It was too dark to see much, but if a shadow flitted through the trees then Sam would have seen it.

'Follow me,' Sam said.

He clutched Lloyd's arm and led him round to the back of the shed. The garden tools were lying where Sam had left them, but he had to let go of Lloyd's sleeve to pick them up. He started heading towards the trees, and a minute passed before Sam realised that Lloyd hadn't moved. He ran back for him.

'Lloyd, you've got to follow me. I can't hold onto you. My hands are full. Do you understand, Lloyd?'

In the darkness, Sam couldn't tell whether Lloyd had nodded or shaken his head.

'Come on. Stick close.'

Sam stepped away from the shed and this time Lloyd followed close on his heels. The trees were densely packed on this side of the grounds, which Sam thought was a good thing. Even if the man did see them, it would be hard for him to follow, and impossible for him to know which tree they were hiding behind.

It was cold, and the cold bit through their coats, through their clothes, and through their skin right down to their bones. They needed fleeces, and woolly hats, and gloves, and boots. Maybe Lloyd had been right and they should have stayed in the shed. It had been much warmer in there, in their snug little cubbyhole. It was too late to go back now, Sam thought. Or was it? No, it wasn't. But ... To go back was almost like admitting defeat, and Sam didn't know if he'd have the courage to leave the shed again, especially in daylight. He felt more vulnerable in daylight. It was true you could see everything, but everything could see you.

Sam headed on straight through the trees. He couldn't see the fence yet, or even where the trees ended, but he knew it was only a matter of minutes before they reached the perimeter. He hefted the shovel over his shoulder and wished for the hundredth time he could swap it over into his other hand. His rucksack was weighing him down too, but he was reluctant to get rid of anything in it just in case he needed it later.

Unlike the other side of the grounds where there was a space between the end of the trees and the fence, here the trees went right up to the fence, which was why Sam almost knocked himself out on it. He had been looking back to check on Lloyd, who had dropped too far back, and walked smack bang into it. He doubled over as the pain blinded him, and he had to let it abate before he could do anything.

Any other time what had just happened would have been funny. Lloyd would have rolled around laughing and Sam would have felt extremely stupid for a while and then joined in with the laughter. Lloyd came up beside him and didn't seem to find it funny, and Sam wasn't laughing either. He straightened up. Nothing was broken, only a collection of bruises added to the list of injuries, but Sam didn't care any more. They were at the fence.

'Pick a tree with a wide trunk and keep a lookout, Lloyd. I'll start digging,' Sam said. 'If you hear anything whistle, and then hide. Worse comes to the worst you can always climb up a tree and hide there. He'll never think of looking up.

'Um, I can't whistle properly, Sam,' Lloyd mumbled.

'Then hoot, like an owl. There are lots of them in the woods. Hoot twice, that'll be our signal.'

'Okay.'

Sam turned back to look at the fence. It wasn't quite as he had remembered it. He had thought every railing was anchored in the ground, but it wasn't. It was every tenth railing, with a connecting bar running along the bottom of the fence. The horizontal bar was about three inches off the ground, which meant that Sam didn't have to dig too deep. All he needed was another several inches, and they'd be through.

Sam set the shovel to the ground with gusto. He'd never done any digging in his life, but he knew what to do. He just wasn't expecting the ground to be so hard. Solid, compacted earth. He pushed the shovel into the ground and stamped on it to get it into the ground. Then he levered the handle of the shovel backwards. He didn't get much earth out of the ground for all the effort that went into it. Several times, he made the mistake of hammering the shovel into the ground too hard and then he couldn't lever it out. He learnt slowly that moving a smaller quantity of earth with the shovel worked better even though it felt like he wasn't getting anywhere.

Several inches hadn't sounded like a lot, but now it felt like it was miles away. He'd barely scraped the surface.

Then the owl hooted twice.

Sam kicked some leaves over the fresh soil he had exposed and ran back to where Lloyd was hiding.

'What is it?'

'Over there?' Lloyd pointed back to where they had come from, towards where the sheds were.

Sam watched, but he didn't see anything. His watch said ten twenty. It was late. Didn't the man ever sleep? He waited with Lloyd until his watch said ten thirty, and said, 'I think he's gone a different way. We're okay for now. Do you want to take over the digging?'

Lloyd shook his head. 'I-I-I'm sorry, Sam. I can't go out there. I just can't.' He moved closer to the tree, as if the tree was his protector.

Sam wasn't sure what Lloyd meant because where Lloyd was standing was *out there*, but he kind of had a vague inkling and he didn't want Lloyd to get all upset.

'It's okay. I'll do the digging, you do the looking out.' Sam looked up at the tree Lloyd had chosen to hide behind. It was an old oak with nicely spaced branches, and it hadn't lost that many of its leaves yet. 'Good choice, Lloyd. Do you think you can climb it?' he asked.

Lloyd looked up at it. 'Don't know.'

'Give it a go while I'm standing here. I'll give you a leg up.'

Sam linked his fingers together and got ready, but Lloyd didn't move.

'Come on, Lloyd. It's much safer up there than down here, unless you want to help me dig!'

'Your hand, Sam,' Lloyd said pointing at Sam's cut.

'Oh. Yeah. I forgot about that. Thanks.' Sam realised his cut would open up again if he helped Lloyd up that way.

'Okay, I'll bend over and you climb on top of my back. You should be able to reach the first branch. Ready?'

Lloyd nodded. Sam steadied himself against the tree trunk while Lloyd climbed up. It didn't take him long to get several feet up in the tree. Sam had to get back to digging. Time was passing fast. It was almost eleven o'clock.

'Don't forget to signal if you see anything.'

'Sam?'

'Yeah?'

'Be careful.'

'I will.'

The digging went slowly, very slowly. Sam couldn't swap hands because he couldn't use his left hand, and he couldn't use his right ankle, although he had tried, because of his earlier fall. Every now and then he would straighten up and survey his work. He *was* making progress, but literally inch by inch. The hole was still too small to slither through. It had gone past midnight, and

Sam kept digging and scraping the earth back. He hadn't taken a break for ages and his back was screaming with pain. It was a job just to stand up straight without crying out. He was just wondering whether Lloyd had fallen asleep in the tree when the owl hooted twice.

16

Sam hadn't been sure whether the first two hoots had been a false alarm. It was easy to see things in the darkness that weren't really there. When he had gone over to Lloyd the first time, he hadn't seen anything where Lloyd had pointed, but that didn't mean that there wasn't anything there, and Lloyd had a better vantage point now from up in the tree.

Sam looked around the woods. He couldn't see anything at all. He was tempted to carry on digging. The hole was nowhere near big enough for them to slither through yet. He needed more time on it.

Stop dithering, Sam, decide and decide fast. There was a chance that Lloyd really had seen something, so it would be stupid, idiotic, to ignore his warning hoots. Sam decided. He lay the shovel flat in the hole and covered it with leaves again; it concealed the shovel, but he had to stamp down the pile of fresh soil he'd dug up as well. Then he headed over to Lloyd's tree.

It would be safe up there. He could rest while the man went past on his search, and when it was all clear, he could get back to digging. Only then did Sam realise that there was no way he could climb the tree, not without a boost up, or a ladder or something, and he didn't have a ladder.

He didn't have anything. All he could do was hide behind a tree while the man went past, and that was too close to the ground, too close to *his* reach, too close to danger. And that's when his heart started thumping loudly again and his skin began to crawl. It hadn't done that for a while and it came as a shock to Sam. He thought he'd got over that stage. He hadn't realised he was still so scared inside.

'Where is he?' Sam hissed up the tree to Lloyd.

'There's a light, like a torch. It's swinging backwards and forwards through the trees. Somewhere over that way, towards the left.'

Lloyd's voice was disjointed and far away. He was way up the tree, way out of reach. Sam wanted to be up there too. He jumped and managed to catch hold of the lowest branch. He dangled off it with one hand, trying to swing his legs up on to it. He couldn't do it. He had to use his other hand as well if he stood any chance of making it up. He let go and jumped again, catching the branch with both hands, eyes tearing up as the jolt of pain seared through his left hand and up his arm.

'How far away?'

'Can't tell, Sam. It's moving slowly, I think. I can't tell. Hurry, Sam!'

Sam tried swinging his legs up, but it didn't work. He had to pull up more with one hand and get his other elbow onto the branch so he could lever his body over the branch and then he would be up, and out of reach, and safe. But he couldn't do it with his left hand, the pain was killing him already, and his right arm was aching from the digging. Tears were flowing freely down his cheeks, but he kept on trying, and no matter how many times he said, 'I can do it. I can do it,' he knew he really couldn't.

Sam let go of the branch and dropped down to the ground, panting. A tree had never defeated him before, but he was running out of time. He had to find another one, away from Lloyd, but he didn't know if Lloyd would be all right without him.

'What are you doing?' Lloyd whispered. 'Climb up, Sam. Come and hide with me.'

'I can't get up there. I have to hide somewhere else. How far is he?'

'He's coming closer, Sam. He'll be here soon.' Lloyd had begun to cry.

'Stop crying and listen, Lloyd. You're safe up there. He can't get you. But don't make a sound, not a single sound, until he's gone way past us, and put your hands over your ears, too. We're going to be okay. The hole is almost there and then we'll be outta here. Okay? Lloyd?'

Sam took the little potting fork out of his rucksack and gripped it in his hand, but it didn't stop his hands from shaking.

'Sam? Sam?' Lloyd's voice was wobbling.

'Shush. I'll come and tell you when he's gone. Don't talk any more. Keep quiet.'

Sam had seen the light, and it was coming their way, slowly, in wide sweeping arcs, and Sam thought, I've got away from this before. I can do it again.

He moved into the woods, looking for a nook, a hollow, a low branch, and all the while the sweeping arc of light moved closer. It wasn't just a regular torchlight; it was one of those heavy-duty spotlight lamp things that gave off tons of light and didn't run off just batteries but needed charging. The man must have recharged it during the day so that it was ready for his night-time hunting.

Sam wanted to be able to keep an eye on Lloyd's tree, so he couldn't go too far, but the choice was limited and Sam couldn't see in the dark. As the arcing light got closer and threw shadows and silhouettes into the darkness, Sam spotted a tree that wasn't too far from Lloyd. It wasn't the tallest tree, but its trunk was broad and it splayed off into three hefty trunk-like branches from a few feet off the ground. Its upper branches didn't look that strong, but Sam wasn't going to climb it. There was a niche where the main tree trunk divided into three trunks and that's where Sam was going to hide. He clambered up and squeezed himself into the hollow; it was a tight fit, but that was better in a way. It meant he'd be practically invisible.

The light was coming closer, but at a slow steady pace. Lloyd had been right. The man wasn't going to give up. They might not know his name, but they'd seen his face.

They knew what he looked like, and they knew what he had done. They weren't going to let him get away with it. Sam wasn't going to let him get away with it. The first thing he'd do when they were through the hole was find a police station. If Sam had been bigger and stronger he could have ambushed the man, and knocked him out. Or stuck the garden fork in his leg. Or whacked him over the head with the shovel. That's what Sam wanted to do – and it was a horrible thing.

Somehow, in less than two days, he'd learnt to hate, and it was a hatred so deep that it made him want to hurt someone, kill someone. He'd never hurt anyone in his life. He'd never even killed a spider. But Sam wasn't big and strong. He was just a kid; and he was angry, and he was frightened, and he wanted to go home, that was all.

The light came closer to Lloyd's tree. Sam watched and listened carefully, praying that Lloyd wouldn't make a sound, wouldn't cry, wouldn't whimper, wouldn't answer the man, and wouldn't come down from the tree. 'Please, please, please, Lloyd, don't make a sound,' repeated itself over and over in his head. It all hinged on this one thing, on Lloyd. If Lloyd could hold it together for just a few minutes longer, they'd be fine. They'd be home.

The light went past Lloyd's tree at the same excruciatingly slow, steady pace. Sam ducked down, pressing himself close to the tree, becoming part of it as the light approached him. The man wasn't speaking or calling their names, but Sam's heart was drumming in his ears now and he wouldn't have heard anything anyway. He knew it was worse for Lloyd, but Lloyd had stayed quiet. He'd held it together. Sam had to do the same.

The light didn't pass by quickly. The man was doing a thorough search and he'd carry on searching until he found them. He must have thought they were still there, in the house or in the woods, or he wouldn't still be looking for them, which meant the only escape route was under the fence. The sense of urgency was back and Sam needed to get back to the hole and make it deeper and longer, faster – somehow.

He had to get Lloyd to help him.

But he couldn't do any of that until the man moved on. Why was he lingering around here for so long? Had Sam left anything out in view?

17

The spotlight lit up the woods with its harsh glare, swinging slowly from side to side, but never swinging upwards into the trees. The man was stupid, and they were lucky he was stupid. He was heading in Sam's direction now. Sam scrunched his eyes shut tight. He was close to him now. He could almost hear him breathing. He wanted to stop him from breathing. He wanted to stab the garden fork through his heart so he would never breathe again. But Sam knew he couldn't do it ...Could he? It would have been easy. All he had to do was to jump out of the hollow. The garden fork was already clenched in his hand. It might be his only chance.

Do it, Sam, do it now.

Then the man moved on, past the tree, and the moment was gone.

Sam opened his eyes, but didn't move. He could see the back of the man's head turning from side to side following the beam of light. He took a small step forward and shone the light from side to side again before taking another small step forward. It was a methodical search, a painstakingly thorough search. Was anyone else searching for them with such diligence, with such perseverance? Or was it just the nutter? Maybe everyone thought they had run away. You heard stories of kids running away all the time. Maybe that's why no one else was looking for them.

The man was moving off; he was at least a hundred yards away now and Sam let his body relax and slump down into the hollow. He gasped a breath of air into his lungs, cold air, which made him half-splutter and he had to bury his face in the crook of his arm to stop himself from coughing. You idiot! He screamed silently at himself. Had the man heard? Had he turned back? Sam raised himself up just enough to see out of the hollow. No, he was safe – the man was still going in the other direction, away from them.

Sam waited until the light was well into the distance before prising himself out of the hollow. He had to go and see if Lloyd was okay and then get back to digging the hole. He got out of the hollow with difficulty, and then it took another few minutes before he could walk properly. Cold, cramped, aching, battered and bruised. But there was no time to feel sorry for himself. If he'd been on his own, he would probably have stayed in the hollow of the tree, or in the cubbyhole in the shed, and never have come out. But he wasn't on his own. Lloyd was with him, and he was relying on him.

'Lloyd? It's me, Sam. You okay?' Sam said softly into the tree.

The leaves rustled in the tree and the branches shook as Lloyd made his way down to the lower branches.

'He's gone,' Sam said.

'For now,' Lloyd whispered.

'Look, I need your help digging the hole. It'll go faster with two of us.'

Lloyd looked at him and Sam knew he was too afraid to come out of the tree. He didn't blame him, not one bit. It was the best place to hide.

'He won't come back to this part of the woods for hours. Maybe not until the morning. We'll be safe for ages. You can always come back to the tree.'

Lloyd didn't budge.

'Please, Lloyd. I don't want to be anywhere near here when he comes back.'

After a long pause, Lloyd said, 'Sam ...' and that was all Lloyd said.

Sam wasn't angry with Lloyd. Well, not that angry. If he were in the tree, he probably wouldn't come down either, but he wasn't.

'Hoot twice if you see him coming back,' Sam said, and he turned away quickly so Lloyd wouldn't see the feeling-sorry-for-himself-tears splashing down his face making bizarre tracks through the caked-on blood and mud.

He went back to the hole and scooped the leaves off the shovel. He started digging frantically, blindly, and didn't stop for ages and ages. When he did, his watch said half past five and it was still dark, but the hole was dug and the owl hadn't hooted once.

Sam stared at the hole, not quite able to believe that he'd done it. Raw blisters covered the insides of his hands, and there was a horrible mix of blood and soil all over him, his hair, his face, his clothes; he must have looked like Rambo, or more like a midget orc. But it didn't matter because he had done it. He had dug a hole big enough for a kid to sneak out through.

Lloyd must have fallen asleep while Sam had been digging the hole. Sam had kept half an eye out for the man's spotlight flashing through the trees, but he hadn't seen it. The man must have gone back to the house for a kip – he had to sleep sometime, didn't he? He'd wake up and resume his search and eventually he'd see the hole to freedom, and it would be like a noose around his neck. He'd know he was done for. He'd freak.

Sam pushed his rucksack through the hole and then crouched down on his hands and knees and crawled through the hole, just to check they could get through it okay before he went back to get Lloyd. He squirmed through on his belly and came out the other side. He smiled, and then he went back through the hole into the grounds of the house.

He had to hurry now. It would be dawn break soon and Sam didn't want them to be inside the grounds then.

He wanted to be far, far away from here. He wanted to be at home scoffing a warm bacon buttie with ketchup dribbling down his fingers. The thought of food made him aware of the intense gnawing pain in his stomach. Time to get Lloyd out of his safe house, or rather his safe tree. He ran back.

'Lloyd! Lloyd? I've done it!'

He had fallen asleep, Sam thought, when there was no response from in the tree. He called a bit louder, and then louder again. He had to take the risk. He had to wake Lloyd up. The sky was turning from black to blue, which meant it was almost dawn and it would be light soon.

'Lloyd, wake up! Come on! I've done it. Let's go!'

Finally, the branches began to sway as Lloyd made his way down the tree.

'Sorry, Sam. I fell asleep,' he said when he appeared.

'It's okay. We've got to go. I've finished the hole,' Sam said.

Lloyd peered out of the tree, his eyes scanning the woodland. He didn't seem to sense Sam's urgency.

'Come on. Hurry up. It's clear. He's not around.'

'How do you know that?'

'Because I do. I've been keeping watch and digging. It's safe. Please hurry up, Lloyd.'

Still Lloyd didn't move.

'What's the matter? Don't you want to leave?'

Lloyd didn't reply. Sam stared at him, his mouth open with disbelief.

'How stupid are you!' he snapped, but he was sorry in an instant. 'Come on, Lloyd, don't ruin our chance.'

'I-I just want to be sure he's not waiting for me to come down,' Lloyd whispered.

'He's not!'

'He's going to be really angry with me.'

'It doesn't matter. We're going home,' Sam said. 'He can be as angry as he wants. It won't do him any good.'

'He said he'd take me home today,' Lloyd said.

'What? No, he didn't! And it's Sunday today, and he's not going to take you home.'

'He – he said he would.'

Sam glared at Lloyd. He didn't know what had come over him, or why he was acting so strange. Deep down Sam did know – it was because of the man, and Sam just hadn't realised how much power the man had over Lloyd, or how much of the old Lloyd had been lost, destroyed.

No amount of pleading, coaxing or persuading was going to work when someone was that scared. Sam had to start threatening him, and if that didn't work, he'd have to leave Lloyd in the tree. But that would be the last resort because Sam didn't want to leave Lloyd behind.

'If you don't come down from that flipping tree, *I'm* going to get really angry,' Sam yelled. 'I'll come up there and throw you out of it! I mean it!'

While they had been talking, dawn had broken. Daylight flooded the woods, taking away the secrecy of their hiding place. Their anonymity was gone. The woods weren't that dense at all; they had just looked that way at night. Sam could see the sheds, and the garages further up, and beyond that the big house. If the man had been looking out of a back window, he would have been able to see them. They were in full view. Exposed.

Sam wasn't very good at being angry with Lloyd, especially when Lloyd looked so scared, and he felt awful for yelling and threatening him now. He went back to the coaxing strategy. 'Look, you can see the hole I've dug. He won't catch us. See?' Sam said. 'I promise.'

Lloyd looked at the hole and shook his head. 'It looks too small. I can't get through there.'

'Yes, you can. I've tried it out. Don't be scared. Just come down from the tree. You have to, Lloyd – I don't want to leave you behind. But I will. I'm not staying here. I want to go home. I *am* going home, Lloyd.'

Lloyd didn't move. Sam turned away and started moving off towards the hole.

'Sam?'

But Sam didn't look back; he kept on walking. He heard leaves rustling behind him and the thud of someone jumping to the ground, but he kept walking until he got to the hole. It was completely light now and beyond the fence, Sam could see an open field, knee-high in weeds and brambles. It was going to be hard work getting across it, especially if he had to drag Lloyd along, too. Anyone watching from the house or the woods would see them easily. Stupid Lloyd! If he'd only helped him dig the hole; if he'd only come down from the tree before it got light. But it was okay. None of that mattered now. Lloyd had come down from the tree, and they were going to get away. He waited for Lloyd to catch up.

'You go first,' Sam said when Lloyd reached the hole. 'I'll be right behind you.'

He didn't trust Lloyd to follow him. He could just see him belting it back to his safe tree while Sam was going through the hole, and Sam wasn't going to take that risk.

Lloyd lowered himself down and started squirming through the hole. It was much harder for him as he was a bit bigger than Sam, and Sam wished he'd told him to take his coat off first. Lloyd was struggling and there wasn't much space to manoeuvre inside the hole.

'I think I'm stuck,' Lloyd sobbed.

'No, you're not! Just keep wriggling forwards. You're almost there, Lloyd. Just a bit further. You've done it!'

Lloyd came out of the other side of the hole and sat down facing the grounds. He drew his knees up to his chest, hugging them close, and then he began to rock backwards and forwards.

'See you did it! You're free,' Sam exclaimed with a grin. He was relieved and indescribably happy at that moment.

He'd worked really hard for it, and because of him Lloyd was on the other side of the fence, free of the man, free to go home.

Lloyd should have been happy, and laughing, and smiling, but he had begun to cry.

'You don't have to cry, Lloyd. You're on the other side,' Sam said. 'Right, my turn.'

Just as Sam realised that Lloyd wasn't looking at him but at something over his shoulder, Lloyd raised a hand and pointed into the grounds. Sam turned to look. He already knew who it was.

He must have spotted them when it got light – or he could have heard Sam yelling at Lloyd.

The man was heading down the track from the sheds, coming their way, carrying something under his arm. Something big, shiny and silver.

Sam didn't care. Let him come, Sam thought, and he began to laugh and he couldn't stop, and Lloyd kept on crying, and the man kept walking towards them.

Get a grip, Sam, a little voice said, but Sam heard it through the laughter and the tears. Time to go. He threw himself onto his stomach and started squirming through the hole.

18

Almost there. Almost there. Then he was through the hole. The man couldn't get through the hole – that's why he'd brought the big shiny silver thing with him. Sam knew exactly what it was, and Sam didn't care. He wasn't going to hang around waiting for him to climb over the fence, not when the hole led to freedom.

'Come on, Lloyd.'

Sam yanked his arm, but Lloyd wouldn't get up. He was paralysed; frozen with the fear that came over him when the man was nearby. Sam began pulling and dragging him across the field. They didn't make much progress. Both their eyes were on the man. Lloyd had been *so* right – the sicko just wasn't going to give up. He'd leaned his ladder up against the fence, and he was smiling at them.

What does he have to smile about, Sam wondered. He was going to have to get over the barbed wire and the sharp spokes at the top of the fence, and then jump down this side of the fence. Even for a big bloke like him that was going to be tough. So why was he smiling?

'Wait for me, Lloyd!' he called out. 'I'm coming to get you.'

Lloyd was a quivering wreck by now, and he was doing just that: waiting for the man, and no amount of pulling and yanking was going to get Lloyd off the ground and running away, and yelling at him had no effect at all. Sam didn't know what to do. He knew what he wanted to do – he wanted to run across the field, and keep running for as long as he could. But he couldn't leave Lloyd sitting there, waiting for the man. The thing was the man was banking on that. He knew Sam wouldn't leave Lloyd behind, and Lloyd knew that, too.

The man was at the top of the ladder now. He took something out of his pocket – wire cutters, or something, and started cutting through the barbed wire.

Sam squatted down on the ground in front of Lloyd and held Lloyd's face in his hands so all Lloyd could see was Sam's face.

'Lloyd, listen to *me*, not to him. He won't be able to get across the fence easily. He's got to jump and it's a long way down. There's no way he can do that without hurting himself. If we leave now and just get across this field, we'll be safe,' he said.

He repeated it several times, and finally it did go in. Lloyd stopped crying, but he hadn't stopped shaking.

'Come on, Lloyd. Let's go.'

'I-I can't move, Sam.'

'I'll help you.'

Lloyd shook his head. 'I'm sorry. I'm scared.'

'Don't be sorry. Don't be scared,' Sam said. 'Be upset,

be angry, be anything that helps you get away. That helps us get away!'

The man was leaning over the top of the fence. He'd cut away a section of the barbed wire, but he must have cut himself because his hand was bleeding. He was scowling, and cursing them loudly. They could hear it all clearly. Lloyd cringed and cowered every time he heard the man say his name.

'He's going to kill us,' Sam said quietly.

Lloyd didn't hear him. He was crying hysterically in a huddle on the ground.

Sam dug into his coat pocket, looking for the little potting fork, but he must have put it down when he had finished digging the hole and forgotten to pick it up again. Caught without a weapon again. Then his hand came across the giant glass marble, and he felt its weight. He took it out of his pocket. He'd have to wait until the man was really close before he could use it, but he had no other option. Just one whack, that's all he needed. The weight of the giant marble would do the rest.

Lloyd had started keening now, a horrible sound that sent shudders right through Sam. Sam had never heard anything like it. It was awful. Horrible. A death cry. He couldn't take it. He dropped the heavy marble paperweight on the ground and shook Lloyd's shoulders.

'Stop it! Stop it!' and before he knew what he was doing, he'd slapped his friend hard across the face, and then he did it again. 'I said get angry! Get really, really angry, you stupid, stupid idiot! We could have got away!'

Lloyd went silent and still. Sam wanted to say sorry, but he didn't feel sorry, all he felt was fear now. Then the man's laughter reached their ears. He'd finished cutting through the barbed wire and was standing on the top rung of the ladder watching them. He was ready to come over. It hadn't taken him that long at all. He gripped hold of two railings and stepped off the ladder onto the top horizontal bar that ran the length of the fence. That was the tricky bit.

Sam held his breath. If the man lost his balance now he'd fall, fall all the way down to the ground, and hit the hard earth with a horrible crunch. But he was still laughing and singing Lloyd's name. He was completely mad. Sam willed for him to lose his balance. He was concentrating so hard on it that he didn't notice Lloyd get up and begin walking closer to the man.

Sam ran forwards and grabbed hold of him, but Lloyd shrugged him off easily and continued. Sam grabbed at him again and Lloyd shoved him away hard. He couldn't work out why Lloyd would want to go back through the hole, but that's what he seemed to be doing, and Sam couldn't stop him. Lloyd was stronger and each time Sam tried to grab him, Lloyd threw him off.

The man was still perched on the bar near the top of the fence, leaning forward over the railings, his hands gripping hold of them hard, watching. Lloyd was at the hole now. He ripped his coat off and tossed it on the ground, and quickly squirmed through the hole. Sam made a grab for his legs, but Lloyd kicked out hard, throwing Sam off balance. He hit the ground hard and by the time he got up, Lloyd was on the other side of the hole.

'No! No! No!' Sam screamed again and again, but Lloyd had gone completely deaf.

'Good lad,' the man said to Lloyd. 'I knew I could rely on you.'

Lloyd didn't look up at the man. He took hold of the ladder and knocked it to the ground. Then he went back through the hole and stood by Sam's side. There was an odd glint in Lloyd's good eye. Satisfaction.

The man was as shocked as Sam was.

'You bloody stupid brat! Wait 'til I get down there!' he yelled. He was angry, livid, purple with rage. There was a manic look on his face, and Sam knew if he could have got his hands round their necks right then, they'd both be dead now.

He leaned right over the sharp spiked railings at the top of the iron fence, swearing and cursing. If he lost his balance now he'd be dead, but he didn't. He was coming for them and all Sam could do was stand still and watch him coming. It was too late to run. Too late for anything. And then time slowed down, and Sam saw it all in slow motion. It hit the man square on the forehead. Sam hadn't even seen Lloyd pick the giant glass marble up, but he must have because he'd thrown it and it had smashed into the man's head and come bouncing down to land at their feet. All bloody.

The man wobbled. His arms went slack, and he slumped. He was heavy and the sharp railings did their job. They went right through him.

Sam and Lloyd stood and looked at the man for a long time. Just looking, not speaking. Just making sure.

'Shot, Lloyd,' Sam said quietly, when he found his voice.

'Thanks,' Lloyd said simply.

Sam knew Lloyd played tons of cricket, he just hadn't known what a good bowler he was. He did now, and he'd never forget it.

The boys turned away and headed into the field of weeds and brambles. They walked side by side. At the end of the field was a line of trees and beyond it was an overgrown grassy track. It didn't look well-used, but someone must use it or it wouldn't be there. They could have gone left or right, but Sam took them right. Either direction would have done, though. It wasn't as if they were in the highlands, or on the moors where you could walk for miles and not see a house, or a person, or a car.

'Look!' Sam shouted.

'Where?'

'Over there,' Sam said, pointing down the grassy track. 'What is it?'

Sam began to laugh. He didn't know why it was so funny, but it was. He doubled over with laughter. It wouldn't stop; it kept on going. His eyes began to water from laughing, but he didn't care. He fell to his knees clutching his side. He didn't know laughing so much could give you a stitch. He rolled onto his back, still laughing.

'Tell me! What is it? Sam?' Lloyd said. He was grinning. Sam's laughter was infectious and Lloyd caught it full on.

Finally, Sam found his voice and between fits of laughing, he said, 'It's a blinking lady, walking a blinking dog!'

News Flash

A nationwide search ended when Samuel Parker and Lloyd Fisher, both aged 11, were found safe and well by Mrs. Rose Connaway while she was out walking her dog in a deserted stretch of woodland in Bridgeford Forest. They have now been reunited with their families. The two boys had been missing since Friday afternoon when they were snatched from outside their school by a man driving a white Mercedes.

The man has since been identified as Thomas Craigly, who was employed by the pop group XX as a driver and caretaker of their country home. He had taken the children to the band's mansion in Hertfordshire where he kept them until they managed to escape. The band are currently on tour in the States and have not yet released a statement.

Thomas Craigly's body was recovered from the grounds of the property where he had suffered a fatal accident. The bodies of three children have also been found in graves around the property. They have not yet been named.

Six Years Later

He blew out the candles in one puff. Seventeen was a pretty good age to be, Sam thought, even though his mum still embarrassed him by insisting on baking him a cake. Luckily she had stopped asking if he wanted to invite his friends to his birthday tea when he was fourteen. The birthday tea and the birthday cake were a simple family affair now.

'Did you make a wish?' his mum asked, smiling brightly at him.

'Yes, Mum,' Sam groaned back, in a tone that was resigned to his parents treating him like a kid forever. Then he thought about his wish, and his eyes drifted away, and he forgot he was holding the knife and his family were waiting for him to cut the cake.

'Sam? Sam?'

His dad's voice brought him back to the present. 'Oh yeah, sorry.' He sliced through the cake and set the knife down, grateful that that was over with for another year. It wasn't a big ordeal or anything. It was just that everything was celebrated. Everything. Every tiny little success, or near success, every goal, every run, every wicket he took, or didn't take. Every exam result, good or bad. Everything. And his sister Tab suffered the same indignity, although it was easier on her since she'd gone to Uni. It didn't even matter if Sam failed or didn't do well in an exam because his parents would be kind and understanding and considerate and compassionate – and that was kind of worse than a celebration meal. Actually, it was much worse – especially when he'd gone through that phase of flunking everything on purpose. He'd felt horrible pangs of guilt, and the floods of parental sympathy had almost drowned him.

Anyway, he didn't like to flunk anything any more. He didn't like to fail. So everything was celebrated. And it had been that way ever since ... that weekend.

'Here you go, Sam.' His dad passed him an envelope.

'What is it?'

'Every kid's dream!'

Sam wished with all his heart that his dad hadn't said it quite like that. He wished he'd used different words. Any words. Just not those particular words. They echoed in Sam's mind, layers of memories and carefully constructed shields and barriers fell away reaching back to a distant time that could still feel like yesterday. *Every kid's dream.* Sam's hands suddenly trembled violently. He dropped the envelope. Lloyd would have turned seventeen a few months ago. In February. Sam hadn't forgotten.

Sam had gone back to school a week after that weekend had happened, but Lloyd hadn't come back. *In counselling,* was all his teacher was prepared to tell him. Lloyd would return when he was ready. Sam understood – he had some of that too, counselling, therapy stuff. He couldn't tell if it had helped, but he guessed it must have on some level. It was a shame that the brain wasn't more like a computer. You could select *weekend in September* and then hit the *Delete file* button. Simple. But the human brain wasn't like that, and Lloyd never came back. Then he had heard that Lloyd had changed schools. Sam understood why. He was probably the only one who did. Which was why he'd tried to contact Lloyd, but Lloyd wouldn't take his calls – apart from once. It was just after Lloyd's birthday when he would have got his new top of the range mobile phone from his parents. But neither of the boys mentioned that when they arranged to meet that once, and Sam never asked Lloyd whether he still needed his iPod.

Sam went to see him alone. He knew his way around. He'd made a point of memorising a map of the whole of the south east of England. He knew most of the bus routes, too, just in case. He carried other emergency stuff too, just in case. You never knew, did you? He took the bus to Lloyd's house that Saturday morning. Lloyd's parents were out, which Sam was relieved about because they had met his mum and dad a few times after . . . after that weekend, and Sam didn't want to have to talk about it. Remember it. And he knew that was what they wanted.

They wanted to know everything. They wanted to go over it again and again.

Lloyd answered the door on the third ring. He looked different. The unruly mop of red curls had been replaced by a neat crew cut, but it wasn't that. Lloyd had lost weight – his clothes engulfed him. But at least the baggy style was in. There were dark circles under his eyes that mirrored Sam's. Seemed they both still had trouble sleeping at night.

'Hey,' Sam said.

Lloyd nodded. He opened the door wider to let Sam in, and Sam wondered again whether he was doing the right thing. The house was silent and it made Lloyd's silence feel louder.

'Um, cool house,' Sam said to fill the space. There was a time when Sam would have gawped, but not now. The ultra modern, sleek, minimalism, the huge glass windows and galleries, would have impressed him once. He walked through, following Lloyd's hunched shoulders out into the garden. It was a mild day for March. Spring was almost in the air. They walked down to the end of the garden where most people would have had a swing, or slide, or a tyre hanging off a tree for their kids. Instead, there was a miniature assault course laid out here.

Sam pushed a stone around with his foot and wondered what to say, how to say it. Lloyd was leaning against a tree looking at him. His silence was unnerving. Sam felt like he was looking at a stranger.

'You okay?' Sam asked, unable to bear the silence a moment longer.

'Yeah, great,' was the leaden response.

Sam realised that maybe he shouldn't have come. He should have realised that it was never going to be easy – especially the first time. Maybe it would get better after they'd met up a few times. He shouldn't have brought it with him today though. He should have left it for a while. For a long, long while. Maybe he should have got rid of the stupid thing himself. He didn't have to tell anyone about it and he hadn't. But Lloyd? He had to tell him, didn't he? Or did he? He didn't owe him anything now. They couldn't even be classed as friends any more. The problem was that Lloyd felt like one of his oldest friends.

'Heard you started at a new school. What's it like?'

'Like a school,' Lloyd said abruptly. He must have noticed Sam's discomfort because he relaxed a little when he spoke next. 'Miss the old school though. And the gang.'

'They miss you, too.' Lloyd's old gang were Sam's gang now, but it was different, for them and for Sam. They all felt it. Lloyd's absence had left a big hole, which Sam could never have filled, and didn't even try.

'Still playing loads of footie?'

Sam nodded. 'You?'

'Not so much.'

'We could play at the weekend,' Sam suggested. 'Get everyone together for a game, or something.'

'Don't know about that, Sam.'

'Look, Lloyd, if you want to keep in touch, I'd like that. If you don't, then that's okay too.'

'Dunno, Sam. It's different now, isn't it?'

Sam silently agreed. It was different. It was a bit sad, too, which was why he kept trying. He wanted it to be the same again. The way it had been that first brilliant week of a new school year at the new school, living back in England and knowing that now when you made friends they weren't likely to up and move countries. And when the coolest kid in the class had made friends with him.

'We'll see,' Lloyd finished.

It was weird how grown-up Lloyd sounded. Only six months had gone by. Maybe he'd be okay about Sam giving it to him now. Maybe he'd just throw it in the bin. Still Sam hesitated taking it out of his pocket. He could feel it burning a hole in his trousers. For six months he'd kept it hidden away deep in the back of his wardrobe, wrapped up in a bag within a bag, stuffed inside a sock, in the arm of an old tatty jumper with a whole heap of junk on top of it. Just so no one would find it. And now, suddenly, he was itching to get rid of it. He didn't want it. He didn't really know why he had taken it in the first place. Well, he sort of did know why. He thought he was helping Lloyd. But now, he wasn't so sure whether to give it to him or not. Sam looked away from Lloyd. 'Looks pretty tough,' he said indicating the assault course.

'It is in the beginning. Everything ached. Couple of months of training on it and it's not so bad now.'

Lloyd had been training. Twelve years old and ready for anything. Sam's fingers closed round the little black box in his pocket. Maybe it was the right time to give it to him after all. Lloyd had really toughened up. He was over it.

'Anyway, what was so urgent?' Lloyd asked.

'I've got something,' Sam began, and then he just took it out of his pocket. It was easier than giving it a name. The little black plastic box nestled in his palm. It looked so innocuous. Harmless. It should have contained images of a birthday party with people pulling silly faces at it, or saying daft things. It didn't contain any of those things. Instead …

Lloyd's eyes flickered over it briefly. 'What's that?' he asked, and then he stepped back, flinching as though someone had hit him. His face crumpled up, his eyes disappeared. Realisation had dawned. It was a bleak moment. Sam wished he could stuff the video tape back in his pocket. He wished he'd never brought it here. Why hadn't he just got rid of it himself? Sam's bottom lip began to quiver. He bit down on it. He couldn't look at

Lloyd, so he looked at the ground. He could hear Lloyd's breathing had quickened to short rasps, as though he was struggling to find air. Sam willed the ground beneath his feet to open and swallow him up, or to churn up and carry him high into the sky, take him anywhere but here.

'Where did you get it?'

Sam glanced up at the accusing tone. Lloyd didn't understand. Sam should have explained it all properly before he took it out of his pocket and shoved it in his friend's face.

'From the house. You know – before we escaped.'

Lloyd cut him off, firing his questions off quick and fast. He'd found air and it was Sam's turn to struggle. 'Where? Why'd you keep it? Why didn't you hand it over to the police? Why didn't you tell me about it before?'

'I – I ...,' Sam stammered. Lloyd wasn't waiting for a reply.

'Answer me!' Lloyd growled. His face had gone livid red and blotchy. The anger made it ugly. 'Answer me! Who's seen it? Who've you shown it to? Tell me! Tell me!'

Lloyd bore down on Sam and Sam stepped back quickly, stepped away from the punch. Too late. The right cross connected followed swiftly by a hook across the other cheek. Sam stumbled, stars and black spots danced merrily in front of him, and beyond them Lloyd's fist came at him again. Sam ducked. Too late again. This time he went down and as the sky rushed to meet him, Lloyd loomed over him, fist at the ready again.

Sam had never meant this to happen. He hadn't antici-pated this reaction from Lloyd. He thought he might be upset for a while, but grateful to Sam in the end. None of this was supposed to happen.

'Back off, Lloyd, you're hurting me! Just back off.'

The fist halted mid-flight.

Sam explained quickly, the words tumbling out. 'No one's seen it. No one knows about it. I didn't tell a single soul about it. I just kept it safe so no one would find it, or look at it. So no one would know. I promise you, Lloyd. I wouldn't do that. You know I wouldn't.'

Lloyd's fist dropped to his side. His shoulders sagged as the anger drained away. He sat down on the ground beside him. He didn't look at Sam. His eyes were staring into the distance, looking at nothing. He shook his head slowly. 'Too late, Sam. They know. Everything about that weekend.'

Of course they did, Sam thought. They had got him to tell more or less everything as well. Lloyd had had more to tell. 'Sorry, Lloyd.'

'They said it would help. Help me get over it.' Lloyd laughed. It was a hollow, empty sound. 'Anyway, don't know why you're saying sorry. I'm sorry I punched you.'

'Three times.'

Lloyd looked at him with a ghost of a smile. 'Sorry I punched you three times, Sam.'

Sam held the tape out to him and Lloyd shook his head. 'Don't want it.'

'Neither do I.'

'We'll burn it then, shall we?'

Lloyd went back into the house to find matches while Sam waited. He returned with a pile of newspaper and some kindling.

'We'll barbecue it,' he said, and led the way.

It took ages to light because the weather had been damp recently, but once the wood took it built up a nice heat and everything began to burn. In the middle of the wigwam of wood, the tape melted into a charred black puddle, emitting a nasty smell that clung to the back of their throats. Lloyd prodded the fire with the metal tongs, making sure everything was burning properly.

'It stinks,' Sam said, coughing, but he didn't move away.

'Yeah. It's history,' Lloyd said stabbing at the charred remnants. 'I'll chuck it out when it's cooled down. Don't want Dad wondering why his steaks taste funny.'

'I'd better get going,' Sam said. 'Got a bus to catch.'

'Right.'

Lloyd made no move away from the barbecue pit. 'I'll see you then, Lloyd. I'll call you.'

'Yeah. I'd better stay here until it goes out completely.'

'Okay. I'll shut the door behind me. See ya around.' Sam stuck his hands in his pockets and headed back towards the house.

'Sam?'

Sam looked back. 'Yeah?'

'Thanks.'

Sam shrugged. 'It's okay.'

After that there was silence. No more meetings, no more phone calls. Nothing. Sam had had to give up in the end. He probably wouldn't recognise Lloyd now if he passed him in the street, and vice versa probably.

Best friends for one week six years ago. But Sam still missed him. Strange really.

'Open it then, darling,' his mum said, her hands squeezing his shoulders gently. 'Don't you want to know what's in it?'

Sam ripped the envelope open and pulled out a couple of sheets of folded paper. They had enrolled him at a driving school – two lessons a week. He'd be driving in no time. He turned to the last sheet. It was a receipt for a brand new car. Sam's hands shook a little as he folded up the papers and put them back in the envelope.

'Thanks,' he mumbled, overwhelmed. He stood up and gave them a hug. 'This means a lot to me,' he added. And it did. It meant freedom. *Every kid's dream.*

'You deserve it,' his dad said gruffly, patting him on the back.

'Yes, you do,' his mum said, hugging him hard. Her hand brushed his cheek softly. 'All grown up,' she whispered to herself more than to anyone else. Her eyes had teared up and she sniffed as she reached for her hanky. 'What time was your match, Sam?'

'Three o'clock.'

'Well, eat up or we'll be late,' she said.

Half an hour later he was being driven to his cricket match. His sixth form were playing another college and this was the first match of the season. Sam was on the team. He was a pretty good batsman, a fair fielder, but still couldn't bowl to save his life.

At the club he parted ways with his parents and headed to the changing rooms to meet up with the rest of the team. The college they were playing, Sunningford, was supposed to be pretty good, and one of their bowlers had just signed for a major county cricket club.

'So watch yourselves out there today, or pray to God that he's having an off day,' their captain said.

Sam changed into his whites and hefted his cricket bat in his hands. He was up to bat first. The stands were full; most of the college had turned out to watch, or maybe just to bask in the glow of the first hot, blue-skied weekend of the year. He walked across the green and faced the bowler. Fifty runs later, Sam decided that this wasn't their star bowler and that it wouldn't be long before they made a change. He wasn't wrong.

Ten minutes and another twelve runs later, he faced the new bowler. With that shock of red hair it could have been Lloyd, Sam thought for a minute, and then he wondered what Lloyd was doing right at this moment in time, and whether he even still played cricket.

Sam blinked as a drop of sweat trickled from his brow and into his eye. He wiped his brow with his sleeve and when he looked up the bowler was staring at him, waiting. He nodded that he was ready. He focussed on the ball. And with a clatter the wicket fell. He was out. He hadn't even seen it coming. Still, not bad – sixty-two runs was nothing to be ashamed of. He walked past the bowler on his way off the field.

'Bloody good bowl,' Sam said sportingly.

'Thanks.'

It wasn't just the red hair – there *was* something familiar in the set of his face. Or was it just because he'd been thinking of Lloyd that day?

'Not my best shot, Sam,' the bowler added as Sam turned away.

Sam stopped and looked back, a smile rising to his lips. 'You'll never beat *that* one!'

'Um, catch up with you later? After the match?' Lloyd asked. 'If you want.'

Sam smiled. 'Yeah. You bet.'

Out on the field with the sun blazing down and everything a brilliant green, the past fell back deep under six years of memories, safely back in its little box. The box had been shrinking over the years, and it shrank a bit more that day. It would get even smaller as time went on. Maybe one day it would disappear forever.